EMOTIONS

JUANITA IRVIN

ISBN: 0615726259
ISBN-13: 9780615726250

DEDICATION

First I must give thanks to my heavenly Father for blessing me with the gift and motivation to write.

I want to give a special Thank You to my family for having patience with me. My Husband, Vincent Irvin, My sons Vincent Irvin Jr. & Julius Irvin, my mother, Dorothy Pinkney and my sister Patricia Pinkney.

I want to thank my girls Ida, Eleanor, Vanessa, Kathy, Melissa and Gloria for their continued support, encouragement and for keeping a sister sane.

I'm sending an extra special shout out to Renee Jones, Delores Nelson-Carter, Auntie Veneese and Melissa Harper. Thank you so much for your help and support in making this book a reality.

Most importantly, I want to thank those of you who purchase this book and who consistently support my work. Thank you.

This book is dedicated to everyone who has ever been in an abusive marriage, relationship or encounter, whether it was physical, mental or emotional.

Just remember I can do all things thru Christ who strengthens me. (Philippians 4:13)

By the time the judge walked in, I had lowered my head to say a prayer. As I sat at the table waiting for my verdict to be read, I was nervous as hell.

"Mrs. Anderson will you please stand," announced the judge.

My feet felt like weights as I struggled slowly to stand. I was reminded of all the pain, suffering and abuse I endured over the years. I wondered what would become of my precious Kayla who was only three years old.

I turned and took one long look at my daughter as she sat at the side of Zena. I was hoping this wouldn't be the last time I laid eyes on her.

I knew there would be no way the judge would free me because of what happened to Roscoe. The realization of it all had just settled in. The thought of him abusing me night after night still lingered in my mind. The name calling, the hitting and the countless nights of rape stayed with me. The images were so vivid that I began to quiver.

"Are you okay?" asked the judge as he noticed my sweating and jittery movements.

"I'm fine Your Honor. I managed to say.

"Then let's proceed. On the count of....."

At that moment my mind left me and went over the events of my life that lead me to this point.

Chapter 1

Tayla

"Open your damn legs," are the words that stunned my mind, as the blows came down across my face.

"Please stop. No, no."

"Stop! I'll stop when I'm damn good and finished. This is the least your tired ass can do for me. Now shut up!"

At this point, I was afraid of saying another word or even resisting what he was going to do to me. I knew that anything I said would give him more reasons to beat me, and sexually assault me.

"Turn your ass over."

"No Roscoe please," I cried.

Bam!

A fist came down across my left eye. I could barely move from the pain. Roscoe pushed me over not caring about the blood that spreaded over my face and on to the sheets.

"You better not move," he said. As he held one hand around my neck. Roscoe entered me from behind as I held my breath trying not to scream. I could feel my anus ripping apart. I silently cried from the unwanted physical contact I had just received. Raped by my husband.

How could someone say they love you and do those things to you? A normal person wouldn't treat you in that manner. There were countless days where Roscoe would physically, mentally and yes, sexually abuse me. This wasn't the first time. At this point, nothing mattered anymore, but Kayla. He had taken away every ounce of my spirit, and my soul. I felt I had nothing left but the shell of my body which had become very feeble from the beat downs that were repulsively placed on me.

Roscoe and I had been together for five years. A year after being together we decided to get married. He was everything to me that I hoped a man would be. He was strong, clever, debonair and attentive to my needs. He was a workaholic and believed in taking care of his home. That is, until the beatings began. As soon as we moved, it all started. Roscoe didn't waste any time before he started pounding on me. He started with the name calling, and then the hitting followed. A year later we had our first child, Kayla. I took time off from work to raise our child, but after being back to work for a year I was laid off. Then things took a turn for the worse after announcing I was pregnant with our second child. I thought he would be happy to hear about the pregnancy. I was mistaken. The frustrating thing about it is I couldn't understand why the news of me being pregnant upset him. He refused to talk about it. In fact, he told me to get rid of the baby. An abortion was out of the question for me. So, when I refused to have the abortion, all hell broke loose. He changed. I thought it would only be temporarily. Boy was I mistaken. Roscoe began leaving for days at a time. When he did come home, he would be so drunk. He stopped paying the bills and giving me money. Things were starting to get tight now because he wasn't paying the bills. I wanted to go back to work but I knew it would be hard getting a job with my belly sticking out.

One day when Roscoe came home after being gone for three days. I had no choice but to ask him for money.

"Roscoe, we need to talk."

"There's nothing to talk about."

 "Roscoe, where have you been?"

"That's none of your damn business."

"I'm your wife, Roscoe."

The expression he had on his face told me that I was pushing it, but I had no other choice. Holding up disconnection notices, I said. "Do you see these? The gas and light are going to be turned off."

"Then pay them."

"Roscoe you know I don't have any money."

"That's your damn problem. You should have thought about that before you made that decision."

"You mean the decision of having our baby? We need to talk about this."

"I said I didn't want any more children and that's final."

I didn't know if I should continue. I knew how Roscoe would snap off. This mean disposition and the bad things he was doing to me were getting worse. I wanted to reach him. To make him understand that having a baby was okay. His body language told me he didn't care to hear what I had to say today.

"I'm tired of you bitching all the time. I'm leaving."

Roscoe stormed out the door.

I wasn't sure what I was going to do at this point. I decided to drive over to an abuse support group that my neighbor gave me a pamphlet on. I wanted to check it out. I got myself and Kayla together. I asked my neighbor Ann if she would watch Kayla while I stopped by the support group. She agreed.

***

I drove to the support group and had no ideas that it would be as crowded as it was. There were many women standing up telling their story.

"Hi, I'm Paula I was abused by my husband for seven years. He would verbally and physically abuse me daily. One day he threw a plate at me, and cut me from my left eye, down to my ear. I only have 40% hearing in that ear."

"Hi I'm Beth. I was abused by my husband. He threw gasoline on me and set me on fire."

"Hi, I'm Joann. I was mentally and physically abused by my father. He would beat me daily and controlled my every move."

"Hi, I'm Mary. I was physically abused by my husband. One day he pushed me out of a moving car."

"Hi, I'm Tina. I was verbally, physically, and sexually abused by my boyfriend."

"Hi, I'm Kim my boyfriend would deprive me of food whenever he wanted to control me. He would also pick me up every pay day just to collect my check. The other days I was forced to catch the bus home. If I resisted giving him my check he would choke me and physically abuse me."

The next lady stood slowly still trembling from the thought as her hands traced a trail of scars down her arm. "Hi I'm Nancy. My husband beat me with an iron. He broke my nose, two ribs, and one of my arms."

These stories were unbelievable to me. I became sick by the minute from hearing each woman speak. I was filled with so many emotions that it became hard not to let the tears fall. All around me there were women standing up announcing that their abuse occurred by their husband, boyfriend, lover, father, family member or partner. Many of their abuses ranged from threats of violence, emotional intimidation, economic deprivation and physical abuse. Many of their stories were my story. Each time there was a silent moment. I wanted to jump out of my seat and announce that I, too, was abused by my husband, but I was frozen in my seat. I was too hurt and embarrassed to state what I had been going through. The emotions in the air were very high.

I had heard enough and was getting ready to leave when another woman stood up and announced that she was raped by her husband. I remained in my seat to hear the lady's story as she spoke.

"My name is Ann. I was sexually abused by my husband. He used physical force to get me to engage in sexual acts against my will. I was never allowed to decline participation.

When I was unwilling to participate in some acts he would strike, and kick me causing me bodily harm. There was a time when he broke my jaw and the doctor had to place a wire in my mouth to hold my jaw together."

I ran out of the session and stood against the wall to collect my thoughts before I took my ride home. A woman walked up and asked if I was okay as I was getting myself together. I didn't have to say a word. The lady saw the tears that were streaming down my face.

"I once stood on that same wall as you," she said. "I know it can be hard listening to all those horrible details, but its reality and what all of us have gone through. Getting support is the first step. You're on the right road. You should continue coming to the support groups, and keep looking for help that's out there for you."

I searched into my purse for a napkin to clean my nose.

"Here, I keep plenty of tissue whenever I come here. My name is Zena."

"Hi Zena I'm Tayla."

"Welcome Tayla. Now that we're on a first name basis would you like to talk? You seem as though you could use an ear."

I stuttered on my words. "I...."

Zena grabbed me by the arm not giving me a chance to respond. She led me to a dimly lit room sparsely furnished with a lounge chaise chair and a couch.

"We can talk in here. I have been in this same room a thousand times."

Zena closed the door.

"Please feel free to sit anywhere you like."

I walked over to the couch and sat there. I didn't want to sit on the chaise chair. That would give me the feeling of being in a shrink office.

"Tayla let me begin by telling you that I'm a survivor of domestic violence. I'll begin by telling you about the domestic abuse I went through, and if you want to talk after I finish I'm here for you. If you don't want to talk, at least you will know that you're not the only one going through this and things can change for you. Your life can change by the steps and decisions you make. You have to decide if you're going to deal with it or not. No one can make that decision but you."

I nodded my head as to say I'm listening.

Zena continued, "My abuse started back during my childhood. I was abused by a neighbor who lived in our building when I was seven. This abuse lasted for three years. I tried to tell my family but they didn't believe me. My aunt told me to stop lying because I could mess up Jimmy's life. Jimmy was rubbing on me every chance he could. The last time he forced himself on me. I was in so much pain, and I was throwing up at school. The school nurse was the one that discovered the abuse and reported it to the authorities. Now, this was when my abuse started."

"Zena, you mean your own mother didn't believe you."

"My mother and father were killed in a car accident when I was two by a drunk driver. My brother Bill and I were called the Jones children. We were raised by my grandmother (Mama), and our aunt (Lola). We lived in Bronx, New York. Times were hard back then for the Jones family. Especially, since Mama had to raise two children on her disabilities check. Aunt Lola was also living in the household. Aunt Lola made money in the streets however she could get it. I found out a few years ago that Jimmy paid my aunt, so he could do whatever he wanted to me. My aunt attempted to prostitute her seven year old niece for drug money."

"That's deep. What happened to your aunt?"

"She went to jail along with Jim. She is currently in jail for writing bad checks. I lived in a dysfunctional home, but it was a place I could call home."

"It's unbelievable. So, when did your other abuse occur?"

"Two years ago it ended. I was abused by my husband for seven years. Seven seems to be my lucky number. For some reason I could not leave. Actually, I was afraid to leave. That was until one day my husband beat me until I was unconscious. I barely escaped that beating. The doctors told me that I was one punch away from death. That's when I decided that I had to leave or he was going to kill me. After that I packed up my things and moved away. We didn't have any children together, which made it much easier to leave. I was pregnant three times and had three miscarriages from the beatings. My last miscarriage was due to being thrown down the stairs. These are just a few of the things that I went through. It hasn't been easy by a long shot. The support group has really helped me. I feel that I'm a stronger person now."

"My God, I thought I had it bad."

"Tayla, all abuse is bad."

"That's true."

"Would you like to talk now? I know I just laid a lot of information on you. We can exchange numbers and we can talk at another time."

"That would be better."

"Here is my number, please call me anytime."

"I would love to talk, but I have to pick up my daughter in an hour, and then get home before....."

"I know before your husband start accusing you of being with another man. Been there, done that."

"I want to thank you Zena for this talk. Just hearing your story and how you got out makes me hopeful."

"It can happen for you."

"I hope soon. Things are getting real critical at home."

"You have to make that step, Tayla."

"It's more easily said than done."

"You're right. If you should ever need me whether it's day or night, please give me a call."

"Thanks, Zena. You have made me feel better. I promise if I need you I'll call."

"Will you be coming back for another session?"

"I don't know. Whenever I get a chance I'll try to stop in."

"Okay Tayla. I'll talk to you soon."

I headed out to pick up Kayla. I wanted to get Kayla from my neighbor before Roscoe made it home. I knew he was going to go off on me about leaving Kayla with someone. He would surely think that I was with another man. I didn't want to give him a reason to think that. I knew that I would receive a beat down if that thought was in his mind. He had begun beating on me two to three times a week now. Things were really getting bad and I didn't know how much more I would be able to stand.

Roscoe had told me if I ever thought about leaving him he would hunt me down and kill Kayla and me. This was one of the reasons I never attempted to leave. I knew he meant what he said. So I stayed and dealt with his abuse. There was no one I could talk to. Ann heard the abuse on several occasions, and tried to talk to me about getting some help.

Roscoe would always interfere. He told me he better not see me talking to that lady. In fact he didn't want to see me talking to anyone. I would sneak and talk to Ann whenever Roscoe would be gone for days. Ann tried to convince me to leave, but I remembered the threat that Roscoe threw in my face.

There was no way I could leave, and besides there was nowhere for me to go. I didn't have any income. So, even if I wanted to leave I would not get far without any money.

I thought about talking to Zena the next time I went to the support group to see if there were any houses for women that are running from their husbands. I was hoping that Zena would have some answers for me and a way for me to get out without Roscoe finding me.

I made a mental note to speak with Zena the first chance I got.

Chapter 2

Tayla

I picked myself up off the floor then wiped the blood from my nose. The pain I was feeling was so intense. I tried to make it to the bathroom to see the damage that was done to my face. Once inside the bathroom I noticed the blood that was running down my legs. Immediately, I began to panic. I called out to Roscoe. He ignored me. I buckled over in pain as I tried to go for help.

Roscoe was now sitting in the living room watching a game, and Kayla was taking a nap.

"Roscoe, I yelled.

"What?"

"I'm bleeding, and I need to go to the hospital."

Roscoe didn't respond.

"Please Roscoe. I don't think I can drive."

"So, damn what. That's your problem."

Roscoe continued watching TV. I heard him pop opened his can of beer. Roscoe didn't move. I slowly walked to my room to grab my purse. The pain became even harder and more and more blood shot down my legs. I wanted to call someone for help.

I remembered that Ann had given me her number. I looked in my purse for her number. I dialed her number but there was no answer. I thought about Zena, and hoped that she was home and I could reach her.

I searched in my purse to find Zena's number. I found the number and dialed it right away.

"Hello, may I speak to Zena?"

"This is Zena."

"Zena, I need you."

"Who is this?"

"This is Tayla. I'm in pain, and I think I'm losing the baby."

"Can you make it to the hospital?"

"No, I'm bleeding very heavy."

"You need to call an ambulance Tayla."

"I don't know if I can."

"What is your address?"

"7552 W. Duracell Street."

"I'll send the ambulance to your home then meet you at the hospital."

The phone dropped from my hand as I was passing out, and the sound of a phone constantly beeping began to sound out.

"Tayla," called Roscoe.

There was no answer.

"Tayla," he hollered again.

Still no answer.

Roscoe got up annoyed that I didn't respond. He wanted to know why the phone was off the hook. He walked into the bedroom, and noticed that I had passed out. Roscoe got scared. He grabbed Kayla up and left. He walked out the house in such a hurry that he left the door wide open.

The ambulance arrived shortly after Roscoe walked out the door. They walked right in and began working on me. The ambulance took me to the hospital.

Zena was already at the hospital when they brought me in. Zena informed them that she was a friend of mine. Zena was asked to go to the nurse's station to give them some information about me.

The only information that Zena could give was my name, phone number and address. Zena didn't know anything else about me.

The doctor worked on me. I had lost a lot of blood, and they couldn't save the baby. I was three months pregnant. As the doctor was checking my vital signs I came to. He asked me what happened. He noticed how my face was bruised up.

"I have seen many cases of battered women come into the

hospital."

I didn't respond to the doctor's statement. I turned on my side as the tears formed in my eyes.

The doctor gave his apology about the baby and decided he would let the social worker do her job about the abuse. Dr. Brown was reluctant to leave, but he didn't want to push the issue at this time.

Zena walked in as the doctor was getting ready to leave. The doctor informed Zena that I was going to be okay. Then he excused himself before leaving the room.

"Tayla, what happened?"

I tried to explain how Roscoe jumped on me when I tried to talk to him about paying the bills. I called out to him once I noticed I was bleeding, but he ignored my calls. "I lost the baby."

"I'm so sorry Tayla, but what are you going to do about Roscoe?"

"I don't know?"

"How much more of this are you going to take?"

"Zena, I don't have anywhere else to go. I don't have a job, or any money, and where is Kayla?"

"The ambulance attendants said there wasn't anyone there when they arrived. She must be with your husband. Can you stay with your family?"

"My family put me down when I left home with Roscoe and got married. I haven't talked to them since we moved.

They never liked Roscoe. I don't think any man would be good enough for me to them."

"I'm sure they wanted the best for you. They probably saw something you didn't see about Roscoe."

"Yeah, there were a couple of times when he was a little possessive in front of my family."

"That was your sign then, but we're not going to dwell on the past. We need to make sure this never happens again. Are you going to turn him in?

"I can't Zena. I'm sure you understand?"

"I do. You know that a social worker will be in to talk to you about what happened?"

"I'm not ready to talk to anyone else about what Roscoe did to me. I just want to know where my child is."

"I understand. Remember I walked in your shoes before. Would you like to stay at my place for a while?"

"I don't know Zena. I don't have any money to pay you. Then there's Roscoe. What if he has taken Kayla?"

"You don't know that. Let's get you out of here first, and then we can check on Kayla. I think God is trying to tell you something. You better get out while your life was spared this time. You might not make it out alive next time. You make the decision. You have a few days while you're here to think about it."

"I can't think about me right now. I have to find my child."

"Do you think your husband will hurt your child?

"No."

"Well for the time being she's okay. We'll find her once you're out of the hospital. You get some rest girl. I'll talk to you later."

"Thanks Zena for all your help."

"No problem. Girls like us have to stick together."

I smiled a weak smile before saying, "You're right. It sure would be nice to have someone in my corner."

"I'm here for you Tayla. I know how it feels not having anyone in your life for support. I'm going to be your support system, but for now, I'm going home because I have to get my nap in before work tonight. Do you think you're going to be okay here by yourself?"

"I'll be fine. I don't think I'll have any problems in a hospital."

"Okay girl. I'm out. I'll call you before I head out to work tonight."

"That would be nice. Talk to you later Zena."

"Bye."

I tried to call Roscoe's cell phone after Zena left. He didn't answer the phone. I left a voice message for him to call me back. I laid in bed thinking about Kayla and the baby. I had no idea what I was going to do. I finally drifted off to sleep and woke up when I heard someone in my room. Dr. Brown had come into the room. He had my chart in his hands, and he was standing at the bottom of the bed starring at me.

"I'm sorry I didn't mean to startle you."

This was the first time I notice the sexy doctor. He was very attractive. There was something appealing about him. When he spoke I saw his pearly white teeth, and his hazel eyes that were twinkling when I looked at him. I forgot all about the pain I was feeling as he magnetized me with his sexy eyes.

"I just stopped in to see how you're doing. Are you still in pain?"

"A little Doc."

"I'll put an order in for some pain medication for you. Then we'll see how you're doing tomorrow before deciding on letting you go home. Unless you feel you need a few more days here. Is there anyone else we can call for you? A husband, mother or sister?"

I felt he was trying to see if I was married or in a relationship. I didn't have my wedding ring on. I had to sell my ring in order to pay some of the bills.

"No thank you Dr. Brown."

"In that case, I'll see you tomorrow," he said as he was leaving.

"Okay Doc."

I wondered how I could be thinking about another man. I'm a married woman. It was the thought of being treated like he was concerned that stirred up something in me. I hadn't had any attention from Roscoe or any other man for a long time.

Three days later I was told I could leave. I began to think about Kayla as I was preparing to leave the hospital. Zena brought one of her jogging suits for me to put on. I had left home with only the clothing on my back. There was no sign of Roscoe anywhere. I called home several times and he never answered the phone, or called my cell phone to even see if I was alive. This also made me see that Roscoe didn't give a shit about me. I walked over to the mirror in the bathroom. I looked at the black patch that covered my left eye. I also noticed the bruises that were on my chest and arms. I wanted to cry as I looked in the mirror at someone I didn't recognize.

Dr. Brown walked into the room and saw me looking myself over.

"You're still a beautiful woman Tayla. The scars and bruises will be gone before you know it."

"What about the bruises I have inside?"

"Eventually they all will heal. Look Tayla, I have never done this before, but I was wondering if I could call you sometime?"

I was amazed. The way I looked right now would turn any man off.

"Doc, I'm sure you know I have been through a lot, and right now I need some time to get myself together. If you don't mind, you can leave your number with me."

"You're right Tayla, but I didn't want you to leave here without saying what I feel."

"I'm flattered Doc, but as you know I just lost my baby. I was abused and getting involved again is a long way down the line for me."

"If you need someone to lend an ear, or someone to take care of you, to show you, how a woman is supposed to be treated, then give me a call," he said while placing his number in the palm of my hand before leaving the room.

I wasn't hearing what the doctor was saying because my child was the only thing on my mind at the moment. I was just going through the motions. I began to think about who I could call to see if Roscoe had been there. There was no one. I wondered how I could be such a fool. I didn't have any of his family or friends numbers to call. His family never welcomed me. I always felt uneasy when I was around them. So, I never called their home. If I needed Roscoe, I would call him on his cell phone. I didn't know what I was going to do. I knew I couldn't go back to that house. He left me there to die.

The phone ringing snapped me out of my thoughts.

"Hey Tayla, how are you doing?"

"I'm feeling a little better Zena. Dr. Brown just left here a minute ago."

"You mean that fine doctor that was in your room when I arrived?"

"Yes that one."

"Oh you did notice how fine he was?"

"I'm hurt Zena, not dead."

"What do you think about the good doctor?"

"I'm not thinking anything at all. I'm a married woman Zena. I can't be thinking about another man. The only thing on my mind is Kayla."

"I hear you. I'm going to drive pass your place on the way to pick you up, and see if I see anyone."

"Thanks Zena. That would make me feel better."

"You know that doctor seems to be thinking about you. I saw how he was looking at you."

"He's probably feeling sorry for me."

"No, I think it's a little more than feeling sorry for you."

"Well, I'll never know. I have to get my life together before I can even think about any man."

"I hear you girl. You're right."

"Zena, I was thinking about what you said about me staying with you. Would it be a problem if Kayla and I stayed with you for a while once I get her back?"

"That would not be a problem. I have plenty of room. Besides, I was already making plans for you to stay with me. I think that would be great. I would love the company."

"Thank you Zena."

"No problem I'll see you in a few."

"I'll be ready when you arrive."

"See you then," said Zena as she hung up the phone.

CHAPTER 3

Kyder

I met an Angel today. I could still see her beauty in my mind. Even through the bruises and pain that were repeatedly placed on her. I have been waiting on her all of my life. I know she is the one. I can feel it in my bones. I have been waiting for the perfect woman, and I'm sure she can fit the bill. I have seen several cases where many women have been abused, but none touched me like this one. There was something unexplainable about this woman.

I'm hoping that she would have the strength to leave her abuser whoever he maybe. This lady needs someone to show her how a real man treats a lady.

The individuals that abuse women are savage beast. They have no heart and are very controlling. There is nothing that the women do or say that will ever be good enough for them. They will never change without counseling or some type of anger management program.

They control every moment of the person. They are very

demeaning with name calling. They try to destroy the woman's self-esteem and make her feel like everything that happens is her fault. They want the woman to believe that even the physical abuse is their fault. It's normally never the fault of the woman, but the abuser makes her believe it is.

My only hope is that women stand up, be strong, and believe in themselves. They have to believe in their self-worth, meaning they are more to themselves than anybody else in the world. All women are beautiful whether tall, short, big or small. Women have inner beauty and outer beauty. They have to believe that they are the key to their own happiness by the choices they make. Women need to pay attention to the signs because they are always there. They should never think that because a man is with you they will change. Normally, 80-90% of the time men don't change. Women need to pay attention to how men treat their mothers, or even other women. If they are mean to them, I bet your bottom dollar they will be mean to you.

I state all of this to say that you can change the cycle of abuse. First by developing your self-esteem and self-worth before you get into a relationship. You need to be whole before that relationship, marriage, or encounter can be productive. Secondly, you have to pay attention to all signs whether small or large. There are always signs. Look closely at the man's behavior. Things he is doing now and find out any information from his past. If he truly loves you, he will be open to you and you can learn from how he was brought up and the things and behaviors in his younger life. History is very important. The 90 day rule will give you time to gather information about a person. Don't get me wrong, sometimes it takes longer than the 90 day rule to learn about a person.

Women have to break the chains and the cycle of getting involved with an abusive person. If they still happen to get caught in that web they need to develop the strength to get out or get help to get out. There have been many instances where abuse has lead to death.

I want to help Tayla. I know I can help her. I hope she will be open to my help. Abused women have been treated badly for so long. When a good person comes along they get afraid. If they have to make a choice between a good person and a bad person they will pick the man who will treat them bad. I want to help Tayla change that cycle.

My family is from one of the wealthiest towns in Africa. My father is considered a king and my mother a queen. I guess that would make me a prince. I have so much love and want to spread that love to Tayla.

The boys from my country were raised up to be men. Real men take care of the women in their life. I want the chance to show Tayla how it's supposed to be done.

We want our women to be happy. Our belief is, if women are happy she will make you happy.

The men were I come from are never abusive. This is unheard of. We go out of our way to make our woman happy. We concentrate on her likes and dislikes and we acquire them. We are on a mission to treat a woman like a queen. We pay attention to the little things she likes. We are attentive, pay attention to details, the way we speak to her, our attitude, behavior and enthusiasm all play apart in making her happy and feel like a queen or special.

I know I have my work cut out for me with Tayla, but I'm up for the challenge.

Most of these American women are not use to a good man. When they see a good man coming they don't know how to handle it. They always let the good man go and pick up another man who treats them like crap.

I want to help Tayla change this cycle. If she would just give me a chance. I know she has been through a lot and I will not rush her. Talking to another man is probably the last thing on her mind. I want to be her friend because that's where it all needs to begins.

Tayla will allow me to be in her life if it's meant to be. I spoke with her friend Zena, and she gave me permission to stop by for a house call. I want to check in on Tayla to see how she is healing. I want to give her any help I can. I want her to know that even though I'm a doctor I can be a valuable friend as well.

It hurt my heart to see what happened to her and the loss of her child. I hope that the person that caused her all this pain is caught and placed behind bars for the rest of his life.

Tayla will be healing inside and out for a long time to come. My plans are to help her get through her healing period. I have plans on stopping by to see Tayla today. After I finish my shift I will give her a call even though her friend told me it would be okay to stop by. I'm excited and can't wait to see this Angel again.

CHAPTER 4

Zena

I'm what you would consider Italian and half black. My mother was Italian and she married a black man. I believed because of their union they were never accepted by my mother's family and they struggled and had many hardships. I lost both of my parents at the age of two. My brother Bill and I had to move in with my grandmother and my aunt. There was many times when we were treated mean and different then the other kids in the family. I always wondered if it was due to the added burden we put on the family. My family was poor and feeding two more mouths didn't help.

My life was torn up when I was abused at the age of seven by a neighbor in the next building where I lived. My own aunt attempted to prostitute me to men in the neighborhood. I never knew my aunt was behind it all until I got older. At that age I was thinking about playing with my dolls and jumping rope. Being with a man had never crossed my mind.

The experience was as devastating for me as it would be for any child at that age or anyone being taken advantage of. At one point I stopped talking. Jim had been touching me for three years before he actually penetrated me. He had been touching my private part and putting his private part on me while he masturbated.

I tried to tell but they didn't believe me, and I was told, "If you keep lying on people the police are going to take you away." My family liked Jim because he was always fixing things, or bringing meat and fish to our home. Jim had money, but the bad thing about him is that he liked young children. I found out that my aunt was getting paid to let those things happen to me. It was all terrible and began to get worst when Jim took it to another level. He began to penetrate me at the age of seven. My school was the one that discovered it when I went to school in so much pain. Jim was finally arrested after I went to several counseling sessions and began talking again. I was afraid of talking about what happened because I didn't know what was going to happen with Bill and me. I didn't want to leave my family because they were all we had.

I was convinced that what happened was not my fault and nothing would happen to me if I told the truth. I finally spoke out and Jim was arrested. It then came out about Lola, who was also arrested during this time.

I never knew why Lola was arrested until I was an adult. That was when I found out all the details. It made me sick knowing my aunt was the one that was trying to prostitute me to Jim. It was also discovered that Jim was messing with Bill as well, but he never talked about it. That dark secret stayed locked in the back of our minds. The counseling sessions helped me to be able to deal with it and to have a normal life again.

Bill left home at the age of seventeen. He was four years

older than me when he left. I never knew where he went. Then one day, out of the blue I started receiving letters from Bill. He had begun writing me monthly but he never came back to visit. I learned from his letters that once he turned eighteen he enlisted in the Marines.

Bill could not face returning back to our home town after the trauma he went through. He continued to write me monthly even today.

I lucked up when I turned eighteen and was given an academic scholarship to Spelman College. I felt the scholarship was my ticket to get away from my past.

After graduation I was trying to prepare myself to go away to college. I got depressed when I didn't have any items to prepare. My family was poor and they couldn't help me out in anyway.

My school counselor Ms. Ward really liked me and she looked out for me. Ms. Ward brought me a lot of the items I needed for college, and the school donated some of the things for my dorm room and the school supplies.

There was one more obstacle that I had to face. I didn't know how I was going to get to Spelman. I didn't know anyone that could or who was willing to take me to Atlanta. I surely didn't have money for a plane or train ticket.

Ms. Ward finally volunteered once she saw there was no other way for me to go. She didn't want me to miss out on the opportunity of a life time. Ms. Ward also felt that I needed a new start. I had been through a lot.

So the plan was that Ms. Ward and one of her friends were going to drive me to Spelman.

August came so fast and I was really getting excited. I had all of my things packed in boxes and ready to go. I didn't know what to expect because no one in my family has ever went to college. Ms. Ward tried to fill me in on what to expect and things to look out for. Of course, I was advised about studying. She also had a talk with me about the boys at Morehouse.

At this time I didn't have any encounters with any boys. What Jim did to me was still in my mind and having a relationship with someone was the last thing on my mind.

Ms. Ward also warned me about peer pressure of doing things like drinking, drugs, and yes sex. I didn't want to talk about that subject. Ms. Ward figured I needed to hear it anyway.

The day arrived when I was leaving for college. My grandmother gave me a big hug, and kiss. She also whispered in my ear that she was very proud of me trying to make something out of myself, and she told me she loved me. I was surprised and tears flooded my eyes. It made me feel good to hear my grandmother say those words.

I said, "I love you mama."

I know Mama wanted to say I will write you, but she never learned how to read or write. I always read her mail for her after my aunt Lola went to jail.

I wondered who would be the one looking after my grandmother now that I'm leaving. I only hoped that my cousins would step up and help Mama out and not take advantage of her.

I knew it was too late to think about all of that now. I had to do what was best for me this time. I knew that going away to college was best, and once I finished I would be able to take care of Mama.

I grabbed my last box and gave my grandmother another hug before walking out the door.

As I walked outside and took in the morning fresh air, I smiled to myself. The relief of leaving all of my bad memories behind came to mind. It was as if a new person stepped out of my body, and was announcing "I'm free."

The voice of Ms. Ward calling my name brought me back to reality. "We need to get moving," said Ms. Ward.

I put my last box in the car and got in the back seat.

The ride to Atlanta was going to be a fourteen hour drive.

I settled in the back seat and took out the material that Spelman sent me about attending the college. I had read the material several times, but for some reason I felt I had to read it again.

Ms. Ward was talking to her friend Melba as she drove. They both began to tell stories about their college life and how much fun they had. Ms. Ward and Melba both were graduates of Spelman. So they were able to give me a lot of good information that would be helpful.

Ms. Ward talked about the sororities at Spelman. I listened to the stories and wondered if I would fit in and pledge one of them. Ms. Ward told me that belonging to an organization would be good for me and there are some benefits as well.

I thought about what they were saying and took it all in my mind. There was so much information that I was given that I was beginning to feel a brain overload.

It was now three hours into the drive and I decided to take a nap so that I could be fresh when we arrived on campus.

I felt like the ride was taking forever. I had never been on a trip or rode in a car for more than an hour. Finally we arrived on the grounds of Spelman. It was so crowded with people and cars everywhere. Today was the date that freshmen were allowed to move into the dorms.

Ms. Ward drove to the dorm where I would be staying. Once she parked the car we had to go inside to get a number. The number was the order in which you could bring your things up on the elevator. People were standing outside or sitting on the grass waiting for their number to be called.

I was hoping my roommate had arrived. I talked to her on the phone and wrote her several letters. My roommate's name was Tina. She didn't live in New York. Tina lived in Boston.

My number was finally called. Ms. Ward had located a dolly to place my things on so we wouldn't have to make several trips and for the heavy items.

We moved all of my things into my room. I arrived before my roommate and picked my side of the room.

Ms. Ward and Melba helped me to unpack and get my room in order. Then they took me to the grocery store to get food for my room. I was all settled in when my roommate arrived.

When Tina stepped into the room we screamed and hugged each other like we have known each other for years.

Ms. Ward informed Tina and her parents that we were going to eat dinner at six and asked if they would like to join us.

Tina family agreed to meet us for dinner.

"Come on Zena. Let me give you a tour of the campus and show you where your classes will be held. Then we can go purchase your books," said Ms. Ward.

"Okay." I'll see you later Tina.

Ms. Ward showed me all of the important buildings on campus and what rooms my classes would be held in.

I thanked Ms. Ward and Melba for all their helped. I felt Ms. Ward was like my godmother, and I was glad that Ms. Ward took the time to help me out.

By six o'clock everyone was ready for dinner. We ate at the Golden Corral Buffet with Tina and her parents. We all enjoyed our dinner and the parents were ready to go to their hotel rooms and relax. It turned out that Ms. Ward and Tina parents were staying at the same hotel.

They dropped Tina and I back off at our dorm room. We were still full of energy and ready to get busy walking around the campus.

Tina was a social butterfly and she was ready to open up and explore college life.

***

Several years passed. My college life turned out to be a wonderful experience. That is until that dreadful day. In my third year of college I was date raped by a boy that lived in Atlanta. After that incident I could not go back to school. I left Spelman and moved back home. I struggled to get myself back together. It was hard for me and I kept on blaming myself for the rape. The abuses I encounter were hitting me hard and I refused to even leave the house.

I thought college was my chance of having a normal life and

now it was all taken away. I felt my life would never be normal again.

Chapter 5

Roscoe

Life for me wasn't easy. My family lived in the ghetto all of my life. We never stayed at one apartment very long due to my mother running and hiding from abusive men. She never was involved in a stable relationship now that I think about it. There were never any positive or supportive men in our life that I could look up to. As for my father I never knew him. I was told he never was in my mother's life. The minute she informed him she was pregnant with me he left. She never heard from him again. I think that is one of the reasons why I never wanted children. What is the purpose of a father anyway when the mother does everything? I never knew the man that I should have called daddy or father.

Mama tried to do the best she could by raising us. I'm sure it became hard for her after having seven kids by different men and no fathers around to help. I believe my mother did the best that she could.

I had seen a lot by growing up in the ghetto. There were many things as a child I should have never been exposed to. There were lots and lots of prostitution. The pimps were always beating up on their girls and they didn't care who saw it. It was nothing for them to smack them around, blacken their eyes, and bust their nose or lips. I saw this activity at least two or three times a week. We would all watch in amazement how the pimps were running their business right before the eyes of young boys.

I've seen people laying in the streets with needles stuck in their arms, boys stealing food because they hadn't eaten in days, and the list goes on and on and on.

I had to deal with being beaten by several of my mother's boyfriends. I was even raped by one of them when I was eight. I never told that to anyone. It just seemed that my life got worse and worse after that. I stopped going to school and hung out in the street with the older boys. There were several times when I went to jail. I wasn't doing drugs or selling. I was just hanging with them, but because they were I was booked for selling narcotics. It all looked good to me and I wanted the money and action they were receiving.

I also started having sex at a very early age. I believe probably well before I even knew what I was doing. My sexual experience started out with an older woman named Kitty. She opened my eyes up to the world of sex or should I say "nookie" as we called it back then. Man Kitty was advanced. She showed me some moves and let me practiced them on her often until I got real good.

I also learned to hustle on the streets around the same time I met Kitty. I wasn't good at hustling so I didn't stay in the game long.

Dealing with the women was my thang. I became good at

being involved with them. I developed my player skills at an early age and became good at it as well. I was running game in every area of my life.

There were some people who would say I was a little crazy in the head but to me it was survival of the fittest.

Everyone knew I didn't take any shit off of women, and I had plenty of them. I was in control. I wouldn't say I was a pimp, but I was close to it. I had many women taking care of me and all of my needs. They were only my women not women of the streets. That's why I wouldn't say I was a pimp. My women couldn't be with any other men. They were strictly mine.

I taught them to anticipate my needs and to listen for key words of things I wanted or needed them to do. I didn't have to tell them anything. I just sat back and let them do what they do.

All of that was cool for a minute. That was until the women began to trip because they wanted to tie me down. I wasn't ready for one woman and I let them know that up front.

I never did hard drugs. I only smoked bud. I remember that one day I was getting high with some friends and I began to trip out. They said I was jumping all over the place and talking out of my head. I began banging on the walls and doors and was trying to jump out the window. My so called friends had to call the police to take me to the hospital. They put me in a psych ward and labeled me as a schizophrenic. I was put on medication that I stopped on my own. I didn't like the way it made me feel. I never told anyone what the doctors labeled me but my mother. From time to time I would still trip out and have those strange behaviors or delusions.

Then my mother would always say, "You need to take your medication." I would start back taking those damn pills for a while, but eventually I would stop taking my medication. My mother kept it a secret for a long time and I was able to live a normal life. Well, a life I would call normal. I was always able to hide my problem very well from everyone, but my mother knew the real deal.

I never let my little problem keep me down. There was no way I could show to everyone that something was wrong. I continued with my life as if I didn't have a problem. I was a functional schizophrenic if there is such a word. There were many times when my body and mind just wanted to break loose and do its own thing. I would be staring into space and my body would have this strange demeanor. Nothing in particular would set me off. It was just the way my mind had begun to work. Life went on for me despite what I was going through. I believe I was getting better and better every day. I would have forgotten that I have a problem if it wasn't for the medication I was taken.

As long as I took the medication I was in control of my life. The medication became a natural part of my life. I began to take it daily as it was prescribed for me. Then I began to date again but it was very hard for women to stay with me or for me to have a long relationship. The women never knew about my little problem but some of them would leave just as fast as they came into my life.

I got tired of women turning me on then deciding that they didn't want to be with me anymore. So, I started to take control of the relationships. To show them who was the "man" of the house.

I knew I was very insecure and controlling, but I couldn't help what I had become. My environment created me to be who I am, and this has been the story of my life. Even up to the point where I met Tayla.

CHAPTER 6

Tayla

Zena was telling me little bits of her life each time that we got together. She continued the story by telling me that after college it took her three years to get herself back together. She went to counseling sessions and a support group to help her deal with all the abuse she encountered in her life. She felt she had become a better person from the help that she received. Zena said it wasn't easy, but she didn't give up.

She knew she had to get herself together because her grandmother (Mama) was not doing well. Mama had several mini strokes and was admitted into the hospital. That was when Zena began to worry because things were not looking good for Mama. She was worried about her grandmother and how she was going to make it if she should pass away.

There was no money coming into the house, but Mama's disability check. That check would surely be gone if something was to happen to Mama.

Zena told me about a time when Mama was talking to her before she went to college. She told Zena, "Go to college and make something out of yourself. Don't let your past keep you from moving forward with your life. Be strong and never depend on anyone. Get everything you ever want in life on your own. You will become a better person that way. God bless the child that got its own."

Zena said those words stayed with her. She spoke the words to me like Mama said them to her yesterday. Zena said she understand now what Mama was trying to tell her. Mama was telling her that she wouldn't be around forever, so she has to make a life for herself because there was no one else out there to help her anymore.

Zena said when Mama told her that she began to think about how she was going to take care of herself if she passed away. Zena said she thought about it every day and she knew she had to come up with a plan, a roadmap to build on her future.

Her first plan was to find a job. She told me she searched the wanted ads in the newspaper. She thought about babysitting and decided against that job. Zena didn't want to clean shit or be bothered with crying babies. She also thought about checking with Ms. Ward to see if she knew anybody who was hiring.

Zena said she knew she had to do something and she had to do it fast. She finally decided to go down to her old high school and talk with Ms. Ward.

Zena said she woke up early. She was ready to get busy putting her plan into motion. After getting dressed her plan was to go to the hospital first. She took her shower and dressed up in a business suit. She was preparing herself for looking for a job after visiting with Mama. Zena said by nine o'clock she was dressed and ready to walk out the door. The visiting hours at the hospital didn't start until 10:00 a.m.

She walked out the house and to the corner where she had to wait on the bus to take her to the hospital. Zena stated that forty-five minutes later she was walking into the hospital. She went to the patient information desk and asked for her grandmother's room. She was given a pass and headed to the elevator.

Zena pushed the button for the second floor. Mama was in room 2209 of the intensive care unit.

She got off the elevator and looked on the wall to see which direction to go to Mama's room. The odd numbers were to the left of the elevator.

Zena headed that way. She found Mama's room and went inside.

Zena said with teary eyes, "Mama is still in a coma and breathing on a respirator. She wanted to cry from seeing all the tubes and machines that were connected to Mama. Then a nurse came into the room to check the machines. Zena asked her if there has been any improvement. And her answer was "no change." She also talked with the doctor. She asked him will her grandmother get better. His response was "it's hard to say. We have done everything that we can do. Now it's up to God."

At that point, Zena said she moved closer to her grandmother's bed and grabbed her hand, and before she could get a word out the tears streamed down her face. She then told her grandmother, "Mama, its Zena. I love you Mama and please come out of this coma. I need you."

43

Zena said she remember laying her head on Mama's chest as she wept. There still was no change or even movement at this time. She continued to talk to Mama hoping she could hear her. She said, "What am I going to do without you Mama. I don't think I can make it without you. Please wake up Mama."

The nurse came into the room and heard Zena crying. Zena held up her head when the nurse walked around to check the monitors. She told Zena, "You shouldn't give up on your grandmother. God has not given up on her."

Zena looked at the nurse as she realized what she had just heard. It was true. God hasn't given up on Mama she thought, so she shouldn't as well.

Zena tried to collect herself because she had just heard something powerful. She then made up in her mind that she wasn't going to give up until God said it was done. She wiped at her tears and bent down and gave Mama a kiss. She told Mama she would see her later because she was going to look for a job.

Zena thanked the nurse for her encouraging words and headed out the door. She turned in her visiting pass and walked out the hospital and headed toward the bus stop.

Zena got on the bus that led her to her high school. She needed to have a talk with Ms. Ward about finding employment right away.

After thirty minutes Zena landed on her high school grounds. She went to the main office and asked to speak with Ms. Ward. The secretary in the office remembered Zena and chatted with her for a while before allowing her to go to Ms. Ward's office.

Ms. Ward was sitting at her desk when Zena knocked on the door. Ms. Ward was happy to see Zena. They began to chat for a while before Zena informed her of the reason she came by.

Zena told her that Mama is in the hospital. She is very sick, and the doctors are saying it's in God's hands.

Ms. Ward told Zena to let God do his will. God doesn't make any mistakes and he will take care of her. Ms. Ward went on to ask Zena how she was doing.

Zena stated that she was doing well.

Ms. Ward reminded Zena to be careful and to remember that some friendship and acquaintances can lead to date rape. She told her she has to be careful with the people that she meets and with them offering her drinks. Alcohol is very often involved in date rape.

Ms. Ward handed Zena a pamphlet about date rape. The pamphlet stated that, "Drinking loosen inhibitions, dull common sense. Drugs may also play a role in date rape.

The date rape drugs are rohypnol, gamma-hydroxybutyrate, and ketamine. These drugs can be easily mixed in drinks to make a person blank out and forget things that happen. People that have been giving these drugs reported feeling paralyzed, having blurred vision, and lack of memory. Mixing these drugs with alcohol is very dangerous and can possibly kill you."

Ms. Ward showed Zena a part of the pamphlet where it talked about ways to protect yourself. It stated, "To avoid secluded places until you trust the person you are with, don't spend time alone with someone who makes you feel uneasy or uncomfortable. This means following your instincts and removing yourself from situations that you don't feel good about, stay sober and aware. If you're with someone you don't know very well, be aware of what's going on around you and try to stay in control, know what you want. Be clear about what kind of relationship you want with another person. If you are not sure, then ask the other person to respect your feelings and to give you time. Don't allow yourself to be subject to peer pressure or encouraged to do something you don't want to do, go out with a group of friends and watch out for each other, don't be afraid to ask for help if you feel threatened. If you're injured, go straight to the emergency room, call or find a friend, family member, or someone you feel safe with and tell them what happened, if you want to report the rape, call the police right away. Preserve all the physical evidence. Don't change clothes or wash, write down as much as you can remember about the event. If you are not sure what to do, call a rape crisis center. If you don't know the number, your local phone book will have hotline numbers."

Ms. Ward wanted to make sure that Zena knew this information. She didn't want to give her the pamphlet and let her throw it in a corner somewhere. So, Ms. Ward went over the information with Zena to make sure that she heard it and understood it.

Zena thanked Ms. Ward for the information. She then asked Ms. Ward if she knew anyone that was hiring.

It turned out that the school had an opening. Ms. Ward went to check to see if the position was still available. After twenty minutes she came back to her office and informed Zena that the Assistant Clerk position was still available. Ms. Ward talked to the Principal about Zena filling the position. The Principal was more than happy to offer the position to Zena. She was told the position was only ten dollars an hour, but it's a start.

Zena was so excited. She thanked Ms. Ward for all of her help over the years.

Ms. Ward told Zena to go to the office and complete the necessary paper work for the position and she would be starting on Monday.

That's how Zena got her first job.

CHAPTER 7

Tayla

I was so interested in the rest of Zena's story. I wanted her to tell me all the details about how she came to Brooklyn. She told me that Mama passed after being in a coma for three months. She had already had everything arranged and put in place. Mama knew that Lola would never do right or be able to take care of the business. Everything was already paid for and written out. The only thing Zena had to do was take the obituary to the printer.

Somewhere down the line Mama put Zena as the beneficiary over her policy. The policy was enough to pay for everything that Mama wanted and there would be enough left over for Zena as well. Zena never knew about this until Mama passed and she was thankful that Mama thought about her.

Zena also found a letter that was addressed to her attached to the life insurance policy.

"*Dear Zena: If you are reading this letter then I must have already passed. I had Sister Prueit from the church to help me write this letter out to you. I left everything in place to make it easier on you. You didn't need the added stress of trying to arrange my funeral so I took care of all the necessary arrangements. Please know that I loved you very much, and I know in the beginning it was hard trying to adjust to our way of life. I'm sorry for all the things that you endured and went through. I wish I could have protected you better and kept all harm from you, but as you know you can't take back the past. So, be strong and remember that none of those things were your fault. You have to let go of the past in order to build on your future as I told you before. I also knew in my heart that you were a strong person and I believe you will make it far in life. After everything is done you should have a little nest egg to get you up on your feet. I want you to remember that God bless the child that got its own. I also want you to always remember the Serenity prayer. God grant me the serenity to accept the things I cannot change, and courage to change the things I can and the wisdom to know the difference. If you can remember those two things then you will do well in life, but most importantly I want you to know that I love you!*

Love Mama

Zena cried after reading the letter Mama wrote to her. The words were touching and would stay embedded in her heart forever. She folded the letter that Mama wrote to her and held it close to her heart. She was relieved that Mama put everything in place.

Zena's brother came in for the funeral, but immediately left back out after everything was over. He couldn't deal with being in that house or even in the city. There were so many bad memories that he couldn't deal with.

Zena stated she wanted to make Mama proud and take care of business from this day forward.

Zena worked and took care of the house over the next few years. Everything was going good for Zena, but she had no social life. Some of her co-workers tried to get her to come out for drinks on several occasions. Zena would always decline the offer.

Then one day she decided she wanted to go out. She was tired of sitting at home alone. One of the staff at the school was leaving, and they were having drinks after work for that staff. Zena was asked as always to come out. This particular day she accepted. All the staff was happy and surprised that she was going.

They liked Zena. She had a likeable personality and she was fun to be around. Zena was maturing. She thought that she should be able to have some fun and take care of business when she needed to.

After work everyone headed down to Klub Karma. This was the regular spot for some of the staff.

Zena rode with Chloe. She still did not have a car, but had it in her plans to purchase one soon.

They arrived at Klub Karma and went straight to the bar. Her co-worker Chloe likes to sit at the bar. Zena remembered her saying when you go out sit at the bar. Men always come to the bar to purchase their drinks. That way you're sure to catch the eye of someone you would like to talk to.

There were plenty of seats at the bar due to it being early. There were ten staff that came to the club and everyone was able to sit at the bar.

Everyone was ordering their poison, and their choice tonight was shots of Patron. Zena didn't know what to order. It had been a while since she had anything to drink. Chloe tried to get Zena to have a shot. Zena felt she wasn't ready for that yet.

Chloe ordered two shots as each of the other staff ordered theirs. She passed one to Zena. Everyone begin to make a toast to Donald as they held up their drinks.

Zena followed suit and did the same with the shot Chloe passed to her. It took Zena two swallows before she could finish her drink, and she was almost choking once she finished. Zena couldn't handle the shots. She told Chloe that she thought she was going to stick with the Apple Martini's.

Zena thought Klub Karma was a nice club. She liked the atmosphere and the coziness of the club. She said the music was sounding good to her. Zena looked onto the dance floor and watched different people who were dancing. She got excited from watching the people dance and wished that she could learn how to dance like them. Zena was fascinated and couldn't keep her eyes off of who ever stepped onto the dance floor.

Chloe saw how interested she was in watching the people dance, and she told her that if she is interested the club offer dance lessons for stepping on Wednesday nights. They only charge five dollars for the lessons. Chloe handed Zena a plugger that was on the bar about the stepping class.

Zena looked it over then placed the plugger in her purse. When she looked up a man standing at the end of the bar was smiling at her.

Zena was shocked. She looked around to see if he was smiling at someone behind her or someone standing next to her. There was no one else there. She asked Chloe if she thought the man at the end of the bar was smiling at her. Chloe told her, "You better know it." He still continued to smile even when Chloe was looking. He didn't have any shame in his game, and he was very confident. He knew what he wanted, and it was Zena.

By this time he walked over to where Zena was sitting. He introduced himself and asked Zena if she would like to dance. She declined the offer, and told him that she was not a stepper. He also informed Zena about the classes that Klub Karma offered. Zena told him that she might check into the class. He introduced himself to us as Eric.

Eric asked Zena if it was ok to join her for a while. Zena offered the empty seat next to her. He offered Zena a drink which she accepted. She requested an apple Martini this time.

Zena said Eric was a very attractive man. He was about five feet eleven and had a medium brown complexion with gorgeous eyes. He was also a nice dresser.

Zena thought there was something hidden behind those gorgeous eyes of Eric. She just couldn't figure it out.

Zena and Eric continued to talk together for the rest of the night. The conversation was good. Zena said Eric had her laughing all night. She was really enjoying his company and the music. So much that she hated to leave. It had been a long time since she heard the voice of a testosterone person talking just to her. She loved the attention he gave her.

They talked about family, and Zena didn't have much to say. She let Eric do all the talking. She mention to Eric about the death of her parents and Mama.

Zena found out that Eric was an electrician and he had many skills under his belt. He was married once and now he is divorced. Eric has one child that is five years old. He told Zena that he is a work alcoholic, but he tries to find time to get out from time to time.

Zena thought maybe he was trying to hide behind his work to make up for his divorce.

They continued to talk until two in the morning until the club closed.

They exchanged numbers and said their good nights to each other.

On the drive home Chloe asked Zena what she thought of Eric.

Zena stated that she thought Eric was nice. He's definitely good looking, provides a good conversation, and he's funny. There is something about him that she couldn't put her finger on. She thought he has some nice qualities, but she wondered is that enough?

Chloe was hoping that Zena would give him a call. She knew that Zena needed someone in her life.

They talked about Eric all the way to Zena's house.

CHAPTER 8

Zena

I finally told Tayla how I met my husband and how the abuse started with him.

It started when I was sitting at home listening to music one Friday night. I was sitting up in bed with a book in one hand and my wine glass on the table next to my bed.

I was feeling mellow and wished I had someone to talk to. I thought about Eric. I got up and grabbed my purse. I pulled the plugger out of my purse because he had written his number on the back of it. I looked at the clock and noticed that it was nine o'clock. I wondered what Eric was doing as I ran my finger over his number.

I wanted to call him so bad, but I was afraid. I didn't know what the phone call would lead to.

I picked up the phone several times then put the receiver back down. I stated that after drinking several sips of my wine I finally got the nerve to make the call.

I dialed Eric's number and waited for him to answer the phone.

He was surprised that I had called him. We talked for hours that night. We made plans to meet at Klub Karma. I was going to take the stepping class this Wednesday. I gave him my address and told him he could get my phone number off his caller ID. I also gave Eric my cell number.

Eric told me he would pick me up around six-o'clock. The class starts at seven. His plan was for us to get there a little early so we could have a drink. He told me, a drink usually loosen you up before you start dancing. It gives you a little added courage.

I told Eric good night and I would see him tomorrow.

Eric picked me up the next day as he said he would. He took me to the steppers class and I had a good time. I said the class was really nice and it could be thought of as an exercise class. The instructors really give you a work out. I could tell by how my hair was soaking wet.

I continued going to the class every Wednesday. Eric continued showing up as well. He even began to work with me on stepping. I was picking it up fast and loving every moment of it.

Eric and I were talking on the phone constantly and spending time together. Eric was always the perfect gentlemen. Several months passed and Eric and I began to get closer. I felt I finally found someone to love me. Eric had fallen in love with me as well. He asked me to marry him seven months into our relationship. I accepted. I didn't want to be alone any more.

Eric and I got married. We were so happy. Everything was going good and Eric continued to make me feel good about myself and treat me like a queen. It was amazing because life with Eric was wonderful.

That is, until one particular day when Eric came home from work in a very bad mood. Everything that I said to him seems to set him off. He was yelling at me and criticizing me. It was so bad that he brought me to tears. Every day it began to get worse and worse.

I was so surprised. It was like another person had taken over his mind and body. I felt like he wasn't the same person anymore.

I was thinking it was because of the pressure from his job. So I didn't put too much into it. I felt it would work itself out, but it never did. I knew that I didn't deserve how he was treating me. Then it got worse as the days and years passed. It got so bad that Eric began to physical, mentally and sexually abuse me, and I was afraid to leave.

It was hard for me to believe that a man who was so loving and kind could turn into a beast like Eric did. I always thought there was something hidden behind his eyes, but there never was any signs about anything abusing or anything else for that matter.

I hung in there hoping he was going to change. Then I got pregnant and Eric changed back into his loving self for a while and out of the blue he snapped again. His behavior made me think that he was bipolar and that he needed to be on some medication.

This time Eric punched me in the stomach and made me loose the baby. I still didn't leave him. I continued to stay year after year, beating after beating, and through the lost of three babies. The last miscarriage was due to being thrown down the stairs.

Seven years into the marriage I was beaten so bad that the doctor told me I was one punch away from death. That is when I left.

One morning I got up and decided that if I stayed he was going to kill me. So I gathered what I could and left while Eric was at work. I took all of my important documents. I knew I would need to start over. This was one thing I learned from going to a support groups. I found the support groups to be very helpful. I wanted to help other women that were going through some type of abuse.

I told Tayla that the support group taught me if you are going to leave make sure you have all of your important papers and ID's. It would be very hard to start over without important documents like your birth certificate, social security card, driver license or state ID, passport, school records, bank cards, check book, account information, medical records, and any card numbers you think you may need. You should start gathering this information prior to leaving and keep them in a safe place somewhere or at a family or friend's house if you are afraid to keep them at home. This little bit of information can be beneficial to a new beginning.

This is when I moved to Brooklyn. I didn't think Eric would look for me there. I had saved up a little money and I had a savings account that Eric didn't know about. My statements were only revealed online. The money I got from Mama was gone. Eric went through that like water once the abuse started.

The move to Brooklyn took almost all the money I had. I only had money left to rent an apartment for three months. I tried to get into the school system in Brooklyn, but there were no openings. I continued to look for employment elsewhere and there was no Ms. Ward in Brooklyn to help me this time. I had to cut off ties there right away, so that Eric wouldn't find me.

I was looking in the want ads one morning and saw an ad from Red's. I went down there and checked out the show. This is how I got into dancing at Red's. I had to live and support myself somehow. I was never going to go back to Eric or live on the street.

I later found out that Eric was missing. No one knew where he went. I just hoped that he is was not trying to find me.

Chapter 9

Zena

"Tayla, I went by your apartment and no one was home. A lady on the first floor said that the man and his child moved out."

"That probably was Ann. Oh my God!

"Roscoe took my child and I don't know where they are."

"Don't worry Tayla. I'm sure we'll find them."

"I hope so. I don't want my baby staying with that monster."

"Have faith. It will work out."

Zena drove me to her home. She lived all alone in a five bedroom house. It was very beautiful and roomy.

We pulled up into Zena's driveway and I was amazed by her home. "Wow Zena your house is beautiful. I know it must be very expensive? How could you afford a house like this?"

"I do have a job Tayla, and I make very good money."

"May I ask what do you do?"

I wanted to tell Tayla that I was a stripper at Red's, but I decided not to reveal my line of work right now. There were times when I would make five hundred to a thousand dollars a night. I was hoping once Tayla got better and her bruises healed she would think about stripping as well. The money was good and it would help her get on her feet. I knew she needed a job. So I decided to be honest and tell Tayla what I do for a living.

"I strip at Red's."

"You're a stripper?"

"I like to think of it as a dancer. There is good money in dancing."

"What about all those men looking at you, and touching on you?"

"Those same men are paying my salary. You don't have to do anything you don't want to do. You can just dance and go home or you can do side dancing and really get paid."

"I don't think I could do it."

"When I started I was scared too. I didn't have a choice. I left my husband and dancing was the only option I had at the time to support myself."

"I hear many stories of women stripping, and how they get hooked on drugs."

"Those women are providing sex in addition to dancing. I only dance. I'm not into drugs or the sex acts. We need another girl down at Red's. One of the dancers left. You should really think about it. It's good money Tayla. You have the looks and the body."

"I don't know Zena."

"Just think about it. Once you're feeling better you can come down and check it out."

"I'll do that."

"Let me show you to your room."

I showed Tayla the room she would be staying in. Then we went into the living room to chat.

"Tayla I'm going to one of the group sessions. Would you like to come?"

"I don't think I'm ready to attend a session right now. I need a little more time. You go ahead. I'll stay here and watch a movie, read a book or something. It's been a while since your abuse. Why do you continue to go to the sessions?"

"The sessions have really helped me to get my self-esteem back. I also volunteer my time there to give support to women who need extra support with their abuse."

"How do you manage the sessions and dancing?"

"Actually, it works out well. The sessions are scheduled for different times throughout the day. I pick the times I'm available to volunteer. I don't start dancing until 10:00 at night."

"I see."

"Tayla, what are you going to do about getting your things from your home?"

"I would love to go by my apartment when I know Roscoe is at work, and grab my things and my car."

"I don't have a problem taking you when you're ready.

Remember the lady on the first floor said they moved out."

"I'll believe it when I see it. Thanks again Zena. Do you mind if I take a nap. The medication I was given before leaving the hospital has me drowsy."

"You go ahead and rest Tayla."

***

Later that evening I was getting ready for work. I showed Tayla some of the costumes I use for my performances. She thought they were beautiful. Tayla didn't know if she could see herself wearing clothing of that nature.

"Who picks your costumes, and dance routines."

"I pick my costumes and make up my own dances."

"I use to be a good dancer, but I haven't danced in some years. Once I met Roscoe I stopped going to the clubs. He said that type of atmosphere wasn't good for a lady."

"Tayla you do know that every word spoken by a man doesn't mean it's right."

"I know Zena. I was in love and I wanted to make him happy."

"Was Roscoe going out?"

"He would go out and have drinks with his buddies."

"It seems like Roscoe was trying to keep you locked up while he went out getting his groove on."

"I don't know girl. I didn't have friends here like he does."

"Did his friends ever come to your apartment?"

"No, but they would call and ask him to meet them for a drink. It was always John or Mike calling. He said they were old school buddies."

"It seems strange that they never came over to visit."

"Roscoe didn't like company at the house."

Zena was thinking that something else was going on with Roscoe. She didn't want to bring out what she felt about him yet.

"I'm going to head out now. I'll see you about seven or eight in the morning. Maybe when I come in we can go by and get some of your things."

"That would be great."

"See you later Tayla. Make yourself home here, and I don't mind if you answer the phone. There's a call coming in that shouldn't be missed."

"Okay, I'll take a message for you."

Zena laughed to herself. "Later girl."

Twenty minutes after Zena left her phone rang.

Dr. Brown was on the line.

"Hello, may I speak to Tayla?"

I wondered who would be calling me.

"Who's calling?"

"This is Dr. Brown."

I was surprised that the doctor would be making a house call.

"This is Tayla."

"Hello Tayla. I was calling to see how you're doing."

"I'm feeling a little better doctor. I understand that it will be awhile before I'm fully recovered."

"Yes, it will take some time. I hope you're taking it easy and giving your wounds time to heal?"

"Yes, doctor I am. Do you always make house calls?"

"No, but I was very concerned about you."

"How did you get this number?"

"Your friend slipped it to me and said it would be okay if I wanted to check on you."

"I see."

"Are you getting ready for bed?"

"No, I took a nap earlier. So, now I'll be wide awake for awhile."

"Would you mind if I stopped over? I just finished my shift, and you're on my way home."

"Well I…."

"If you're worried about me stopping over at your friend's house, she already gave me the okay."

I thought to myself. "That girl is going to get it."

I didn't know what to say. I'm not sure I would be good

company."

"Let me be the judge of that. I'll only stay for a few. Just long enough to have a cup of coffee and check your wounds. I'll be gone before you know it."

"Maybe for a little while."

"You don't have to worry about putting on any clothes. I've seen plenty of women in pajamas. You should be relaxing."

"Okay doc, I'm sure you have the address."

"Yes, I'll see you in a little bit. I'm on my way."

"I'll be here."

I hurried to the mirror to check myself over. As I looked in the mirror I knew there was nothing I could do fast to make myself look better. I cried to myself for the pain I was feeling inside and outside. I knew that only time would heal my wounds. Nervously, I began to pace the floor not knowing what to expect. Finally, I decided to go into the kitchen and put on a pot of coffee. Then I sat down at the table. My mind was absorbed with everything that I had been through. Then the ringing of the door bell startled me out of my thoughts.

I slowly got up from the table with the feeling of not being sure, if seeing the good doctor or any other man was the right thing to do.

The door bell rang again. I paused for a minute, thinking I couldn't leave the doctor standing outside ringing the bell. I did give him permission to come over. Besides, he didn't appear to be leaving anytime soon. I opened the door with a half smile on my face. I felt there was nothing for me to be happy about. I wanted to abolish all men at this time.

The doctor was standing in the doorway with a perfect smile on his face showing all thirty two of his perfect white teeth.

"Hi, I thought you fell asleep."

"I'm sorry. I was in the kitchen and I didn't hear the doorbell with the water running," I lied.

"Is it okay to come in?"

"Oh, I'm sorry. Please come in," I said opening up the door. I led the doctor into the living room.

"Please, have a seat."

"Thank you."

"Would you like that cup of coffee now?"

"Yes, that would be nice. Maybe it will help to relax me. I just completed sixteen hours at the hospital."

"And you're still doing house calls. You must be tired?"

"A little. You were en route to my home. So, it's not a problem at all."

"Let me get your coffee. How do you like it?"

The doctor looked at me before he responded. He was making a house call, but it was more personal for him.

The look he gave me showed in his eyes. I could read his every thought. He wished he could take me in his arms and make love too me. Although he knew he couldn't move to fast. He knew what I had just gone through. He didn't want to scare me away. The doctor wanted to show me how a real man treats a woman.

"Black, I like my coffee black," he finally said.

I went into the kitchen to get the doctor a cup of coffee. When I returned he had turned off the TV. I handed him his coffee, then took a seat.

"Do you mind me turning off the television? The news is depressing to me."

I was hoping the TV would give us something to talk about other than me.

"Would you like the radio on instead," I asked.

"Quietness would be nice, but if you prefer the radio I wouldn't mind."

"I'll turn the radio on low." I hoped the dusties would help to perk me up.

"That's fine. How are you healing?"

"I'm not sure."
"Sit here. Let me look at your wounds," he said tapping the seat next to him.

I sat next to the doctor so he could check out my eye and my bruises.

He grabbed his black bag and searched for his instruments to look into my eye. When he found the one he wanted. He softly and delicately tilted my head back to see if any damage was done. When he finished he looked over my bruises, and just the mere touch of him sent chills up my spine. I quickly began to shiver.

Dr. Brown felt the shiver and asked, "Are you cold?"

"Not really. I just got a little chill."

"Maybe you should have a cup of coffee. It would warm you

up."

"More like keep me up."

"What about some tea?"

"You're right. Some tea would be good. I'm not sure if we have any here. Let me go and check."

I'm sure the doctor was glad that I was leaving the room for a minute as well. I felt he wanted time to readjust himself. I was really waking up the man in him. I know he didn't want to scare me off.

I wanted any excuse to get away from under his gentle gesture of comfort for a minute. Even though I had a little shiver, his touch was quickly warming me up. In fact, I was getting ready to sweat. The walk to the kitchen would definitely cool me down. What is going on I thought? I found the tea and made a cup. I went back into the living room. The doctor had fallen asleep. I didn't know if I should wake him or let him be. He was holding his cup of coffee in his hand. I went over to release his cup before it hit the floor. The doctor woke up from the sudden movement of the cup being taking out of his hand.

"I'm sorry I dozed off for a minute."

"I understand. You just finished sixteen hours at the hospital. Do you think you need to be getting home?"

"Not unless you're ready for me to leave."

"I don't want to keep you from your rest."

"Sitting here talking to you is rest enough. Let's talk for a while before I leave."

I wiped at my brows because I had begun to sweat.

"Tayla, are you okay? Now you're sweating. You seem to be going through some changes here."

"I know doctor. I don't understand it myself."

"Are you feeling okay?"

"I feel fine."

"Maybe you should stop by the clinic and get a full check up."

"I'll make an appointment tomorrow, Dr. Brown."

"Good."

I was now sitting on the opposite end of the couch. I didn't want to sit too close to the doctor. Something weird was happening to me. Something I had never experienced with Roscoe.

"Please call me by my first name, Kyder."

"Kyder? How unique."

"That name was given to me by my grandfather."

"Does your family live in New York?"

"Only my aunt. I came here to complete my residency. Then the hospital offered me a job and I have been here every since. I have only been here for three years."

"So have I."

"Is your family here?"

"No. I don't have any family here."

"No one?"

I knew that I would have to explain eventually the events of my life.

So I decided to start with the current events. "Kyder, I was abused by my husband."

"Your husband?"

"Yes, my husband."

"No woman deserves to be beaten by a man. I'm so sorry. Is there anything I can do for you?"

"No, but he has my daughter, and I don't know where they are."

I began to cry.

Kyder came over to me. He held me.

"Don't worry Tayla. I'm sure your daughter will turn up. Have you informed the police?

"No, I can't do that."

"Don't worry everything will be okay. I'll help you in any way I can."

Kyder held on to me and we both fell asleep.

Chapter 10

Tayla

Kyder and I woke up to the sound of keys rattling in the door. It was seven in the morning and Zena was arriving home after being out with her man. She hadn't talked much about him to me.

"Well, good morning," she said with a smile on her face as she looked at me and the doctor.

"I'm sorry. I didn't plan on staying this long."

"No need to apologize Dr. Brown. I'm sure your company was helpful to Tayla."

"Yes Kyder. Thank you for coming by."

"It was my pleasure Tayla. I must be going now. I need to get home, shower and change clothes for the evening. If you don't mind, maybe we can get together later. I'm off from the hospital today."

"Why don't you give me a call later, and we'll see how I'm feeling."

"Good enough. In that case, I'll talk to you soon."

I walked the doctor to the door. As soon as I closed the door Zena began asking questions.

"Girl, you kept the doctor here all night! You guys must have really clicked. Details girl."

"There's not much to tell. We talked, drank coffee and tea until we fell asleep."

"Then the conversation must have been good. He's coming back later."

"I told him we'll see. I don't know if I'll see him later or not."

"And why wouldn't you see the good doctor?"

"As I told you before, I have other things on my mind."

"Well let's start with you going to get your things. Do you think you're ready to do this?"

"I'm not ready, but it has to be done. So it might as well be now."

"Let's go then."

I showed Zena where I lived. We went to my apartment and gathered up as much clothing for Kayla and me as we could get. I put some of my things in Zena's car and the rest in my car. Once we got out of the apartment safely we decided to meet back at Zena's house. Zena got in her car and decided to wait until I pulled off. Thank God she did because as I was getting in the car Roscoe came up and began banging on my window. Zena was watching from across the street. Roscoe had no idea that she was there. She looked up and saw him. Zena was making movements like she was going to faint or she was sick or something.

I had no idea what was going on with her as she left me in danger. I looked over to Zena hoping she was coming to my rescue. Zena had a look on her face as though she was afraid to move. At this point I decided not to bring any attention to her. If she was scared, then I didn't want to get her involved. I finally managed to pull off from Roscoe. I left him standing in the street screaming, and calling me names. Zena snapped back to what was happening before her eyes and pulled off as well, but in the opposite direction. She was driving like a manic. I could see Roscoe turning around to see why someone was driving in that manner. He tried to see who it could be. The car had sped off so fast. I don't think he was able to tell.

I drove to Zena's place still nervous from the encounter with Roscoe. I was still wondering what in the hell was happening with Zena. Did she have a flash back from all of her abuse, I wondered.

I made it to Zena's home and sat in the car to collect myself. Zena pulled up shortly afterwards. She sat in her car as well for a minute. Finally, Zena got out of her car and walked over to me. "That was your husband?"

"Yes, my abusive and controlling husband, and he didn't have my daughter with him either. Hey, what was going on with you over there?"

"I don't know. For some reason I was frozen and I could not move. My own abuse flashed before my eyes. I thought I was over that." I tried to change the subject in order that Tayla wouldn't sense that I was lying.

"Well, the good thing is that he doesn't know where you're

staying. So, you're safe from him harming you."

"Yes, but I don't know for how long."

"Who's going to tell him where you're staying?"

"No one."

"Then don't worry about Roscoe."

"I'm sorry for putting you through that. Seeing him act like that must have really shaken you up?"

Zena was sweating and looked like she was angry. She didn't say anything else as she helped me carry my things into the house.

Her phone was ringing, but it appeared that Zena was trying to avoid answering the call. I took it as she was mad with her man. She had mention before that they were having some kind of problems. Zena acknowledged that something was going on with him and she was trying to figure it out. She didn't care to comment on what was happening. Whatever it was the discovery was too much for Zena to handle.

"Tayla I have to run out for a few. I'll be back shortly."

"Okay Zena. Is everything okay?"

"Yes, everything is fine. I have something I need to take care of. I'll be back soon."

"See you when you return. I'm going to organize my things while you're gone."

"That's cool," said Zena as she headed out the door.

As I was putting my things away the phone rang. Kyder was on the phone.

"Hello Tayla."

"Hi Kyder."

"How are you feeling?"

"Much better."

"That's good. What are you doing?"

"Zena took me by my apartment to get my things. I'm trying to organize them. I don't want to clutter up her place."

"Would you like some help or to go out for dinner tonight?"

"I don't think I'm ready to go out in the public. Maybe after my eye heals and I can take this eye patch off I'll be ready to go out."

"What about me bringing dinner to you tonight?"

"Kyder you don't have to baby sit me."

"That's not what I want to do at all. I enjoy your company. I'm not trying to rush you. A gentleman will wait for a woman. He doesn't rush her into anything that she's not ready for. So, dinner would be fine then?"

"What time do you have in mind?"

"Is seven good with you?"

"Seven is fine."

"I'll see you then."

"Bye Kyder."

Chapter 11

Zena

I drove around the corner and was busy on my cell phone trying to reach Roscoe or Rocky. Whatever his name is. I had discovered after taking Tayla to her apartment that my man and her Husband was the same person. Who would have ever imagined. I was so shocked that I left home to try and reach him on his cell phone. He was trying to call me but I wouldn't answer. I wasn't sure if I could be quiet enough for Tayla not to hear my conversation. I dialed his number. Roscoe answered right away.

"Hello, can we meet today?"

"Zena, how are you?

"I'm fine Rocky. I need to see you tonight."

"I'm not sure if I can meet you tonight."

"Why not?"

"I'm kind of tied up, but I'll see what I can do."

"You never had a problem meeting me before, so what's the deal now?"

"Look Zena. I told you I was tied up. I'll see if I can meet up with you after your show. That's the best I can do."

"Whatever!"

I could picture Roscoe holding the phone in his hand not understanding what was with me.

I ended the call without giving Roscoe the chance to say bye or anything else. I was angry that he had lied to me, and hurt because of what he did to Tayla. I didn't have any idea of how I was going to handle knowing this information. I knew I would have to make time to think my plan through. I decided to head back home. A nap was in my mind and thoughts for how I was going to devise my next move with Roscoe. Tayla had become my girl. I knew that giving up this information could really destroy her and our relationship. She had been through enough already. When I arrived home I barely said anything to Tayla. At this point I was afraid of saying or even being around her with the information I knew. I hurried off to bed telling her I would talk to her later.

"Zena I need to talk to you," shouted Tayla.

"Later Tayla. I'm really tired now."

"I wanted to tell you about Kyder coming over later," said Tayla.

I was in my room with the door closed before she could get it out. I know she wondered what was going on with me. I was acting strange. I knew she would think that maybe she should give me some space and talk to me about it later.

I heard Tayla moving around getting her things together.

Then I heard the water in the shower. I heard her say something about Kyder. So maybe he was coming over again. When I heard the shower running I'm sure she was getting herself together for Kyder. She had mentioned before that she wanted to try and look a little better the next time Kyder came over. After she got out of the shower I heard her pull out a chair in the kitchen. I tried to sleep, but it was the furtherest thing from my mind right now. So the quietness in my room keyed me in to every sound in the house. Tayla was now on the phone. I heard her say.

"What do you mean what the hell I want?" I knew immediately she was talking to Roscoe. I'm also sure that he was verbally abusing Tayla by now. Then I heard her say, "Look Roscoe, let's make this easy for the both of us. I only want to get Kayla and you will never have to worry about me again."

Then she told him, "You don't have to act so ugly and mean and I have never slept around on you so you can stop calling me a tramp. Roscoe, why are you doing this? You know you don't have time to be with Kayla. She needs her mother. Please Roscoe. I want my daughter."

Tayla was crying and stating, "Please Roscoe what do you want me to do? I'll do whatever you want just give me my baby."

I'm sure he was gloating by now. He knew he had Tayla where he wanted her.

Tayla said the words that I never wanted her to say, "Okay Roscoe. I'll meet you. Will you please bring Kayla with you? I need to see my baby."

She finally hung up the phone.

I came out of my room in a hurry. "Tayla, is everything okay?"

Tayla had a look on her face like she didn't know if she should tell me about talking to Roscoe and going out to meet him.

"Zena, I just talked to Roscoe."

"He called you?"

"No, I called him. I tried to plead with him again for Kayla. He wants me to meet him at the apartment."

"Tayla I don't think that's a good idea. You know he's only trying to get you to come to him so that he can beat on you again. What about Kayla, if you don't make it out alive?"

"Zena, why don't you come with me?"

I got nervous. "Come with you. That's out of the question, and you shouldn't be thinking about going as well."

"If I don't go I may never see my daughter again."

"The same may be true if you go. Don't you understand that he's going to hurt you again if you show up?"

"I told him I was coming."

"Well, call him back and tell him that you're not coming. Better yet. Don't call him at all."

"What am I going to do about Kayla?"

"Let the police handle it."

"How am I going to do that? I don't even know where they are."

"I'll think of something, but you can't meet up with Roscoe. Not now or anytime."

"I hear you Zena."

"Good. I'm glad that we got that understood."

"Oh my God I forgot that Dr. Brown is coming back over tonight. Is that okay?"

"Sure Tayla. That's fine."

"You know I owe you for having him to call me?"

"I just thought you needed a little help. No harm intended."

"No harm done. You know it's kind of nice hanging out with the doctor. I haven't had someone to talk to for so long. I forgot what it feels like to have someone to share a decent conversation with. There was no conversation with Roscoe. Lately it was all physical and abusive. Nothing nice."

"Enjoy the ride. It just might be what the doctor ordered."

"We'll see. I don't know where this ride is leading me, but I do think I'm going to enjoy it."

"Who wouldn't enjoy the company of a fine doctor and fine treatment?"

"A person would have to be crazy not to enjoy it."

"Well tonight is yours. I'll be gone all night. So, you and the doctor can have some fun. If you know what I mean."

"Zena, fun I haven't experienced fun in a long time."

"Girl, your body is going to tell you when you're ready to have some fun and when the time is right."

"What do you mean?"

"Haven't you been aroused by a man?"

Tayla confessed. She said she never enjoyed having sex with Roscoe and she never had an orgasm."

"Never?"

"Not even when you made Kayla."

"Not once."

"Girl you have missed out on a lot."

I could not understand why Roscoe didn't please Tayla in the bedroom. I knew what he did for me, and we had great times together. None like I had ever experienced before.

"Zena I thought there was something totally dysfunctional with our whole marriage."

"Tayla, I think times are going to be changing for you. I hope you're ready?

"Ready for what?"

I laughed. "Oh, you just wait and see. Let me get myself together. I want to be gone when the good doctor comes."

I went and gathered up my costume for tonight's show and my overnight bag to spend the night out with Rocky. I'm sure Tayla is wondering why I still haven't told her about him or his name.

I decided I would put in one last round in the hay with Rocky. Then I was going to shake his world up. It was now six o'clock and I was ready to be heading out the door.

Tayla was busy getting herself in some kind of shape so that Dr. Brown could see her in something besides pajamas. She put on a nice low cut summer dress, applied some lipstick and perfume. She had turned the music on low and was waiting for her knight in shining armor who was bringing dinner. The doorbell ranged before I could get out.

Tayla went to the door and let Kyder in. I could see by her face and the twinkle in her eyes that she was beginning to feel Kyder. She was smiling and very happy that he had arrived. Kyder was a well kept man and he always smelled good. He was standing in the doorway loaded down with bags.

"Here, let me help you with some of those bags, said Tayla."

"Thanks, Tayla."

"What do you have in here? Did you buy the store out?"

"No. Just a little of this and a little of that. I didn't know what to bring. So, I brought over several things."

"I'm sure it's all good. Are you trying to fatten me up?" Kyder looked into Tayla eyes. "No, only fill you up."

It appeared that those four little words meant more than just eating to Kyder. They both forgot that I was standing in the room. At that moment my mind took me into thinking about how a real man would fill up a woman mentally so that he would be the only man she think about sexually in order to fulfill all of her sexual desires and physically. He wanted to take care of her for the rest of her life and spend every moment he could with her.

When Kyder spoke my mind flashed back to reality.

"Let's take this food out of the bags and eat before it gets cold. I also brought over some wine," said Kyder.

Tayla mentioned that she couldn't remember the last time she had anything to drink.

Kyder took her hand and looked into her eyes. "You deserve all of the finer things in life, and I would love to give them to you."

My heart dropped just to hear a real man be so real.

Tayla didn't know how to respond. The look on her face showed that she was flattered that Kyder wanted to be with her.

His expression showed that he was intrigued with her beauty. I'm sure that Kyder looked behind Tayla bruises and saw something beautiful in her. He thought she had grace that was hiding inside of her and he wanted to open the cocoon and let the butterfly out.

"We better eat. Let me get some plates down," said Tayla.

This was my key to be leaving. "You guys enjoy yourself," I said as I excused myself.

Kyder began opening up all the food. He had different kinds of dishes. He had Chinese food, Soul food, Mexican food and African food.

"Boy everything smells so good. If I eat from all of these dishes I know I'm going to put on some weight."

"Then we'll walk it off. I love to walk and run in the park. You can come with me to work it all off."

"I'll have to, because I'm going to taste everything that you brought in here. Food is my weakness."

"In that case, we have only just begun. There are a lot of places I would like to expose you to. Remember, I said you deserve the finest. I know some of the finest food places around."

Kyder and I tasted all the food. When we finished eating, we went into the living room to talk.

Kyder wanted to know more about me. He wanted to find out about my abuse and what type of husband I was living with. He wanted to know me and my past history. I knew that talking about my abuse was going to be a touchy subject, but he had to know more.

As Kyder asked me more about my abuse, I completely opened up and told him everything. I had begun to feel comfortable with Kyder and I wanted to be honest with him. I told him everything, down to every episode of my abuse. I told him the story all the way from the first day I met Roscoe.

Kyder felt sorry for me, and for what I had been through. He grabbed me and held me, wanting to protect me from any more harm and abuse.

Chapter 12

Zena

I was getting with Roscoe tonight. I was nervous because of everything that had been going on with him and Tayla, but I felt I had to see him. Now that I thought about it, I knew it was time to put my plan in motion. It was time to make Roscoe or Rocky whatever his name is pay for what he did to my girl. I considered him a disgrace to all women. He was a monster in my eyes and I was going to have some fun while making him pay. With no regrets on how I was going to stick it to Rocky, I prepared myself for our meeting tonight.

Suddenly anger jolted my mind as I was gathering my things for my overnight stay. In addition to my clothing I thought I better pack mace, and my stun gun. I only had the stun gun for men that got out of control down at Reds. You never know what kind of bag a dog is going to come out of. Just in case, I wanted to be prepared.

My plans were to make him trust and love me. Even though, I knew I wouldn't love him back. I wanted him eating out of the palm of my hands. This way it would be easy for me to find out the information about Kayla. My plans were to abuse his love, his money and him mentally. There was no way I could abuse him physically. Rocky was much stronger than me, and for sure he would overpower me.

Continuing with my normal routine with Rocky was going to be hard, but I remembered that I took some acting classes when I was in high school. I had to put on a good performance that would surely be a knock out. I arrived at the hotel a little before Rocky. I wanted to unwind before he arrived. I checked in and went to our room. Shortly after I placed my things down inside the room my phone ranged. Rocky was calling to make sure that I was still keeping with our plans.

"Hey Babe, I was checking to see if you made it to the hotel. I should be there in half an hour. Is there anything that you want me to pick up for you?"

There really wasn't anything that I wanted, but I thought I might as well start putting him to work.

"Would you mind stopping at Kings Chinese food to pick me up some Chicken Cow."

"I'm around the corner from Chinese Kitchen. I can grab you a bite to eat from there."

"Actually, I like King's better. Do you mind Rocky?"

"No problem, but it will take me that much longer to get back to the hotel."

"That's fine. I'm not going anywhere."

"Okay, then I'll see you in a few."

I'm sure Rocky wasn't happy that he had to go out of his way to get the Chinese food. No doubt he was wondering why he was trying to please me. Normally, he wouldn't call to see if I wanted or needed anything. He hadn't seen me in a while so he felt he had to be considerate to get what he had been missing. So, he hurried on his way in order to make it back for some intense pleasure.

In the meantime, I was unpacking my things that I prepared for my time with Rocky. I wanted to do a lot of cuddling and talking during our time together. I laid on the bed and began to reminisce about a time when Rocky and I had a fiery love making experience. The thought was so crystal clear in my mind that my body instantly began to feel the heat.

I began to grasp for air as though I couldn't breathe. My hands became clammy and my body was burning with lust. I struggled to get myself together before Rocky walked through the door. I wished I could enjoy what I was getting ready to do, but I knew it was all business and not for pleasure. My mind kept reminding me about the thrills we once shared. I continued to tell myself that I was doing this for my girl.

Before I could finish reminiscing Rocky was knocking on the door.

"Hello," he said as I opened the door for him.

Rocky placed the food on the counter and walked over to me and hugged me real tight.

"Damn I missed you," he said.

I was Rocky's woman on the side. I knew he was married but never in a million years would I have suspected that Tayla and I would be friends. He wanted to leave his wife several times to be with me, but he never did because of their child. Then he told me his wife was pregnant with their second child which made it even harder for him to leave. At that point I made up in my mind that I was going to get out of this affair.

In Rocky's mind I was going to be the woman for him. The woman he thought was supposed to be in his life. He never got the chance to really tell me how he felt.

Rocky was holding me and he wouldn't let go.

I tried to pull away, but Rocky just held me tighter.

"Hold up! Brother man. My food is getting cold. I'm starving because I didn't have anything to eat today. If I don't eat now I won't have any energy for later."

"In that case, please eat," he said as he released the grip he had on me.

"Thanks for getting the food. You didn't bring yourself anything?"

"No, I ate already. There is only one thing that I'm hungry for," he said, with the look of hurry up in his eyes. Rocky was hungry, but it was not for food.

I sat at the counter taking my time. I ate my food unhurriedly by slowly chewing with each mouth full.

Rocky watched me from across the room. He wished, and prayed that I would hurry up. He was thirsty and hungry for me and he could hardly wait.

I noticed his anxiousness. "Babe, why don't you take a shower and put on something relaxing while I'm eating."

Rocky was silent, but he leisurely got up and grabbed his bag and walked into the bathroom. Cooling off was not something that he wanted to do at this moment.

I smiled to myself. I knew that he wanted me and I was making him wait. I thought to myself that once I take my shower and put on my lingerie, I would climb in bed and work on Rocky. I was going to work on him to get any information that he would give out about Kayla.

Twenty minutes later I turned around as I felt eyes on me. "Oh, you're finished with your shower?"

"Yes, I see that you're finished eating as well."

"I just finished up. Let me go and take my shower now."

Rocky was too threw. He was beginning to feel like I didn't want to get with him.

"What's up Shorty?"

"What do you mean?"

"I'm trying to get with you, and you seem as though that is not what you want? I remember when you couldn't get enough of me."

"Look Rocky. We have the whole night together. I don't want you to get bored with me."

"Girl, if you don't get over here." Rocky was reaching for me.

I gave in for a few minutes so that Rocky wouldn't suspect anything. I kissed him with a long juicy kiss that sent Rocky wild.

"Rocky let me take my shower now, and I'll be out to indulge in some fun with you," I said as I rubbed Roscoe up and down his back.

Rocky got excited from my touch. He wanted me to do whatever I had to do to expedite my return to him.

"Okay baby. Hurry up."

I went into the bathroom and ran a bubble bath and got into the tub. I lingered in the water and fell asleep. I woke up to Rocky tapping me on the shoulder.

"Ooh, I'm so sorry Rocky. I guess I was more tired than I thought I was."

"Come on." Rocky held a towel out.

I stood up and stepped out of the tub. Rocky draped the towel around my body and led me into the bedroom. He began drying me off in a slow stroke motion. Then he got the lotion and massaged my body down. All the while he was getting worked up by looking at my naked body. He watched in amazement at the bumps and curves that were exposed on me. He got goose bumps as he waited in anticipation for what he hoped would come.

At first, I tried to resist the urges that my body was throwing off. I was only human and it was hard to resist the burning desires that were within me. I was not able to fight the advances any longer and I finally gave in. I gave in to the smothering heat that was trapped in my body, and screaming to be released.

Rocky threw down like I knew he could. He relieved me of the pressure that was building up in me.

Once it was over, I moved right into my plans. "Rocky."

"Yes, Zena."

"Look, if we are going to continue seeing each other then we have to be honest with each other."

"What do you mean?"

"Let me be honest with you. Tell me what's going on with you?"

Rocky looked off. He was afraid to tell me the truth. He must think he would jeopardize losing me. Roscoe didn't know if he could stand losing another person. He finally found the nerves to tell the truth. "My wife and I are not together anymore."

"Let's talk about it."

"There's nothing to talk about."

Rocky and I were still lying in bed. I began to rub Rocky's chest. I wanted him to relax so that he would continue talking. I didn't want him to think I was uptight about the situation.

Rocky made up a story about how his wife left him and their daughter. He didn't know I already knew the story. I played along.

"What is your daughter's name?" I asked pretending not know.

"My daughter name is Kayla."

"Kayla, what a pretty name."

I thought how close Kayla's name was to her mother's name.

"And your wife?" I asked.

"I don't know where she is."

"I mean what is her name?"

Rocky appeared to get nervous. "That's not important." He snapped. "I don't want to talk about her."

Rocky sat up on the side of the bed.

I sat up as well and began rubbing Rocky on his back. I felt I was making progress. So, I didn't want to get him angry. I could see this was a touchy subject for Rocky. I wanted to reassure him that I was not mad about hearing his news.

"It's okay baby. I want you to know that I forgive you for not being honest about your family. I'm sure your daughter really needs you right now."

"Yes, she does. Her mother wanted me to give her up, but I don't think she's capable of taking care of her. I couldn't see her raising our daughter alone. She's unstable."

"Let me help you take care of your daughter."

Rocky turned to face me. "You would do that for me?" he asked.

"Yes, I would," I said.

Rocky grabbed me and squeezed me tight. "Thank you. You don't know what that mean to me."

"Baby, I'm here for you, and I want to help you get through this." I didn't know if I was going to pull it off, but I knew I had to try and make it work.

Rocky kissed me all over my face and lips. "Thank you," he said.

"I haven't done anything yet."

"Thank you for offering."

"No problem baby. When do I get the chance to meet Ms. Kayla?"

"Soon, I'll plan an outing for the three of us."

"Great."

Rocky was happy that I wasn't upset, and I was planning on

helping him. He set out to please me after realizing that I was on his side. Rocky wanted to give me what I wanted. He wanted to satisfy me like I was going to please him by helping him with his daughter.

He didn't want to disappoint me. Rocky began kissing me on my neck. I wanted to resist but I couldn't. The feeling was stirring up from the tips of my toes. My toes began to curl up and instantly heat rose in my body. It became obvious to me that I wasn't going to be able to withstand the urges my body was feeling and longing for.

I held my composure a little longer, while in my mind I was screaming for another round with the "Rock."

Rocky continued his pursuit by teasing me with his tongue. He could see that I wanted him, but he felt I wasn't ready yet. His tongue glided over my body as he taunted me. He wanted me at the moment when my body began to tremble for him. He was going to intentionally make me wait, in order that we could release our sap together.

I closed my eyes and a moan escaped my lips. I knew that I was at the point of no return. As my body relaxed, I opened up and welcomed the heated contact I was receiving.

I kept telling myself that I had to go with the flow to help my girl. I also thought it was a damn shame that I was enjoying it. It wasn't supposed to be enjoyable for me. Not with my girl's husband. There wasn't supposed to be any excitement in this for me. I knew I had to carry on no matter what I had to do.

Rocky was laying it on me thick. I reached over and grabbed his manhood when I couldn't stand the teasing any longer.

I didn't know what had gotten into Rocky. He was always good in bed to me, but today he was exceptional. Fireworks were on display in my mind as my world was being rocked.

Rocky rolled over after succeeding in his calling. He saw the smile on my face and knew that his mission was accomplished.

I got up and went to the bathroom to take a shower. As the warm water lingered over my body, I thought about how it was a shame that Rocky was a waste of some good sperm. I felt he had potential, but his mental status was not too tight. I was sure that Rocky's true colors would show once everything came out about what he was doing. I knew I had to plan for that as well. I didn't care as long as I was helping my girl get her daughter back. We would have to stick together. Men do it all the time.

Chapter 13

Tayla

Kyder and I had begun going out. He informed me that he had some time that he was getting ready to take from the hospital. Kyder wanted to spend some time with me. He wanted to take me away for a while to get my mind off of what I have been through. Kyder had a private jet and he wanted to fly me to Hawaii for a few days. He informed me of his plan.

I was excited. I had only been to New York and my home town of Atlanta. I had never been on a plane and now I was getting ready to be on a private jet. I had a week to get myself together. Zena was helping me pick out a wardrobe to take on the trip. She had to lend me some of her things. She said she didn't want her girl going away looking like she was homeless. Zena told me to plan on having a good time because once I return I need to start thinking about making some money.

"I'll check out Reds when I come back. I can't promise anything about stripping, but I'll come down there and see what it's about."

"Fair enough Tayla. You go on your trip and you have a good time. Don't you worry about anything. You deserve this trip."

"I don't know about deserve, but I know I want this trip. I have never been on a vacation before. I have only been to two other places in my life, and one of them is my birth town."

"Well enjoy it while the good doctor is pursuing you."

Zena was happy that I was not thinking about Roscoe.

***

A week later, Kyder was leading me to his jet. I was happy as a school girl on her first date. I was beginning to look like myself again, and I no longer needed to wear the eye patch. I was dressed very nice in my long white summer dress, and my white pump shoes. I was smiling from ear to ear. Something I hadn't done in a long time. I was happy for the moment, but the thought of my child weighted heavy on my mind.

Kyder could see that my mind was always cluttered with thoughts. He told me he wanted to move the dark cloud that hung over my head. He wanted to open me up to new experiences and a new beginning. None like I have ever experienced before. Kyder wanted to expose me to the real meaning of love. He knew if he had my heart the rest would follow.

Kyder took me by the hand and we boarded the jet. I was scared and excited at the same time. He sensed my nervousness and assured me that he would protect me. Not just for now, but for the rest of my life.

We walked onto the jet hand in hand. Kyder escorted me to my seat. Then he asked, "Are you okay?"

I smiled, "A little nervous, but I'll be fine."

"Your first time on a jet right?"

"Yes, this is my first time on anything in the air. I get the feeling that a lot of things on this trip will be my first time."

"Good."

"Good. What does that mean?"

Kyder held onto my hand. "I told you before that you deserve all the finest things in life. You are a wonderful woman Tayla. Life and I have so many things to offer you if you would just accept them."

I needed a drink at this moment.

"Kyder, do you have any wine on board?"

"Sure. I'll fix you a glass."

He went to the credenza and poured a glass of wine and fixed himself a drink as well. Kyder was a Hennessey man. He liked his Hennessey on the rocks. He handed me a glass of Sangria, "Here you are," he said.

"Thanks."

Kyder got up again. "I have something I need to show you." He said excitedly. He went into another room and came back with some pictures. When he returned I was looking out the window. The jet had taken off forty-five minutes ago. I was admiring the scenery out the window. It was the clouds that helped me to relax. I hadn't even taken a sip of my wine. The clouds gave me the peace of mind that I needed at that moment. I had never seen this sight before, how the clouds paraded in the sky. It was a beautiful site to see. Just like a picture. The clouds were like pillows of mountains floating in the atmosphere. It gave me the peaceful feeling of being closer to Heaven.

"Is everything okay," he asked.

"Yes, everything is fine. I'm just enjoying the perfect picture outside."

"I noticed that you haven't touched your drink."

"I'm sorry. I don't think I need it now."

"Well, let me take it for you."

"Thanks. What did you want to show me?"

"Just some pictures of where we're going."

Kyder sat down next to me. He handed me the pictures, then he waited until I looked at them.

I asked, "Have you been here before?"

"Yes," was all Kyder said. It seemed that he was trying not to give me much information.

"Was it business or pleasure?"

"Actually a little bit of both."

"I see."

"Don't get me wrong. It wasn't with another woman, but I have always had plans of coming back with someone special."

"Why didn't you?"

"There was no one special to return back with."

"How long has it been?"

"Two years."

"You mean there has not been a woman in your life in two years?"

"There has not been a special woman in my life for four years, and besides, I never had the time to commit to a serious relationship."

I'm sure Kyder didn't make the time until now. I wondered if that meant I'm the one that he wanted to share every special and passionate moment with. I just hope he will wait until I'm ready. I think Kyder is a patient person. He has been allowing me to be the guide of the relationship. Kyder didn't want to pressure me.

He knows he would have to be patient and he is willing to wait. Kyder wanted this time to be right and perfect. He knew that the only way it could be right was if my marriage was over. Kyder wondered if he could wait that long, and if I truly wanted to end my marriage.

Kyder was in deep thought. I believed he was thinking about what my plans might be. I could tell he wanted to see if he had a chance for a future with me. He snapped out of his thoughts when I asked, "Hey where are you?"

"Oh, I'm sorry. I was just thinking about something I need to take care of."

I'm sure that was not the truth.

"No thinking about work this week," I said.

"You're right. It won't happen again."

Kyder seemed to hold back on what he was really thinking about. He probably wanted to wait it out, and see how everything goes.

"Look, this is what I wanted to show you," he said.

Kyder held up pictures of places in Hawaii. He showed a picture of the home we would be staying in. The home was off the beach.

"Wow, this is beautiful. Whose home is this?"

"My family owns this home. Look at the rest of the pictures."

He handed the rest of the pictures to me.

There were many pictures of different places in Hawaii and different rooms of the house. All of the pictures were beautiful and romantic. Every one more breath taking than the other.

I was so excited and for this moment I was happy. I promised Zena and myself that I would not worry about my problems while on this trip. I would enjoy the hand that I was dealt at this time.

Tears flooded my eyes.

"Tayla why all the tears? Have I done something wrong?"

"No Kyder. You have done everything right. I guess I'm over joyed. I have never in my wildest dreams thought I would be enjoying a trip of this nature with ...."

"Tayla were you going to say something?"

I couldn't finish the sentence. I wanted to say with the kindest, thoughtful and most handsome man in the world. I was afraid. Afraid that I would run Kyder away with my inexperience. I was afraid that I didn't know how to truly love a man. I was afraid of what could truly happen. I now understood that what I experienced with Roscoe was only delusional love.

"I was going to say, I never thought I would be enjoying a trip of this nature with everything that has been going on in my life."

"Never sell yourself short. Life has so much for you."

"I know. You told me that before, but it's hard to believe that anything good would happen for me. I've been in a fog for so long. It's hard to see the light."

"Everything will become clearer. Just give it time."

"Everyone keeps telling me this."

"You have to believe it."

"I know Kyder. That's enough about me. Let's finish talking about this wonderful trip you have planned."

"There's nothing more to tell. I think the pictures speak for everything."

I looked over the pictures again. "There is so much that I have missed in my life."

"Don't worry. I want to show you the world."

"The world?" joked Tayla. "You do know the world is a very big place?"

"Yes, and we will explore it together."

I knew that Kyder meant everything he said.

"Kyder what did you do before you were a doctor?" I asked.

"Went to school."

"How can you afford all of those nice things you have?

Don't you have student loans to pay off?"

"Actually, my family is very well off. My parents paid for me to go to school. At first they were against me going to college."

"Now that's strange."

"What do you mean"?

"I never heard of parents that are against their children going to school."

"Well, my family is very rich. They feel that I can get anything I want without going to college. They didn't want me wasting my time and their money."

"So, why did you go?"

"I wanted a chance to do something on my own. I wanted to earn something for myself. I always wanted to help people. More like save people."

"Is this what you're trying to do for me? Save me."

Kyder took my hand. "Oh no, let me be honest with you? I want you in my life. Not for a companion, but as my wife. I know you have been through a lot. I know you are still married. When the time is right I will be waiting for you. Tayla at the end of the day, I want to come home to you. The first thing in the morning is your face that I want to wake up to. I'm not asking you to make any decision now, but I wanted to let you know where I stand. I'm willing to give you as much time as you need."

I was touched. I wanted to cry, but I held back my tears. I couldn't believe that things were finally looking up for me. I felt as if I was in a fairy tale. I wondered when I was going to wake up. "You can pinch me now."

"This is not a dream Tayla. It's all real."

I thought about everything that was happening. I didn't want to make any hasty movements. I knew there were a lot of loose ends I needed to take care of. Roscoe would be the hardest one. I knew he wouldn't give me a divorce without a fight, and I didn't want to bring any problems to Kyder.

"Tayla let's just enjoy the trip. I don't want you to ponder on what I just said. We'll deal with all of that later. I want you to relax and enjoy yourself."

I was glad that he felt that way. I knew I needed more time before deciding on what to do.

"Are you hungry?" Asked Kyder.

"Yes, what do you have?"

"I have steaks, chicken, chops and fish."

"Is everything cooked already?"

"No, I have a chef who will cook for us. I had the refrigerator stocked for our trip. So, what would you like?"

"I think I would like chicken."

"I'll inform the chef."

I thought that at this point nothing else Kyder showed me would surprise me. I see that Kyder is a man with money who likes nice things. I wondered what Kyder saw in me. There is nothing that I have to offer him. I thought it over, but I could not come up with a single answer.

Kyder walked back into the room. "You're doing too much thinking, relax. I guarantee you'll have a good time. So stop worrying."

"Having a good time with you is not the issue."

Kyder said in his sexy deep voice, "Then what ever it is, let it go. I want you to be free of all thoughts about things back home."

I didn't want to tell him it was him that I was thinking about. Instead I said, "Okay Kyder. I'm going to let it go for now." I felt that when your life is turning and tossing it's hard to make any decisions.

***

Two hours later we were eating a wonderful meal the chef prepared. I enjoyed the splendid meal that was set in front of me. I had chicken with lemon pepper, garlic mashed potatoes, carrots and broccoli. Kyder had steak with garlic mashed potatoes, carrots and broccoli.

Kyder threw in some jokes to lighten up the mood. He wanted to relax me and see me smile. His plan was to make me happy by showing me lots of attention, spending a lot of time with me, traveling with me, and being a real man in my life.

CHAPTER 14

Hawaii

Hawaii was more beautiful then I could have ever imagined. The house we stayed in was like a palace. It was secluded and on a private mountain top. Kyder had maids and servants like he was royalty.

I had never seen anything like it before except on television. I wasn't use to being waited on hand and foot. I was always the one doing the work. A maid was putting my clothes up, running my bath, ironing, washing, laying my clothing out and cooking my meals. The maid wanted to bath me, but I thought that was a little too much. I didn't know if having a servant was something I could ever get use to.

I wasn't use to this kind of living, but I'm sure as hell going to welcome it with open arms.

I was in heaven and loving every minute of it. I couldn't ask for anything more. Just being with Kyder was enough to make me happy.

In the morning Kyder would run on the beach and I would sit out on the rocks looking into the horizon. I was trying to free my mind as I sipped on a nice cup of coffee.

I wanted to enjoy everything that Kyder was offering me. There were several occasions of intimate touching and romantic evenings. Some too close for comfort.

Kyder never pushed. He knew when I was ready my mind and heart would open up and receive him. It would have to be my decision. He was trying to be patient, but I could tell that Mandingo wanted to come to a head. It had been a while for him with all the long hours he was working at the hospital.

One particular night, we took a stroll on the beach. The only light present was the light glowing off the moonlight. A tender kiss was shared and Mandingo did a dance.

Kyder knew that I must have felt him because I immediately jumped back. Mandingo had scared me. He knew he would have to be gentle with me. Kyder remembered what I told him about my past sexual experiences with my husband. It was never pleasurable for me. I never experienced an organism, and I had no idea of the real feeling of making love.

He wanted to be my first in everything wonderful that I experience from here on out.

I ended that night early. The look on his face said he wondered if I needed a cold shower as he did.

I had my own room, although there were several nights when we fell asleep together after watching movies. Those nights were pure and innocent.

I was feeling something inside as well. Something I never experienced before. Something strange was happening with my body again, but a little more intense. I was almost weak after that kiss on the beach. I began to sweat all over from head to toe. I even felt the moistness in my underwear. I was soaked to the bone. This was one reason why I excused myself. I thought that something was wrong with me. I wanted to hurry in and take a bath to clean myself up.

This never happened with Roscoe. I would never be moist enough and always had to use a lubricant. Roscoe was the one that stole my virginity. He was the only man I had ever been involved with.

There were other nights when things began to get hot. Kyder was being patient, but he didn't know how much longer he could go on without the prescription that Mandingo longed for and starved for.

On another night, Kyder had to run out to take care of some business. He returned earlier than expected and walked in on me lotioning up my body. His first reaction was to turn and walk away, but he couldn't move. Kyder was frozen in his tracks. He looked on and neither of us said a word.

Kyder was enjoying the beautiful voluptuous site before his eyes. He wondered did I know what I was doing to him. Kyder also wondered why I didn't ask him to leave. I was standing in front of him nude, and the sweet smell of my perfume was calling Mandingo.

Our eyes interlocked after Kyder finished scanning my alluring body. Kyder walked over and gently touched my face. He could feel my heart beat with the touch of his smooth long strokes. As he moved in closer my breath became shallow.

I closed my eyes, as I was filled with mixed emotions. My cell phone rang as I anticipated Kyder next move. I pulled myself out of my trance, and quickly answered my phone.

Once I reached for my phone Kyder left the room.

"Hello."

To my surprise, Roscoe was on the line. I had not heard from him in a long time.

"Do you think I'm a punk?" He hollered into the phone.

"What?" I said.

"Are you deaf now?"

I held my breath as I held the phone without saying a word. As I was listening, I hurriedly put on my robe. It was as if I knew Roscoe would be walking through the door any minute.

"When I get a hold to you it won't be nice, and you can forget about ever seeing Kayla again."

"Please Roscoe," I screamed.

Kyder ran into the room. "What is it Tayla?"

I put my finger up to his mouth to tell Kyder to keep quiet.

"Who the hell is that? I know you're not with another man. You're more stupid then I thought you were?" said Roscoe.

He went on and on with the verbal abuse. He became extremely indignant. I couldn't take it any longer. I began to cry.

Kyder grabbed the phone and ended the call.

"No," I said.

"I've heard enough and had enough of seeing you hurt. Please don't let him destroy you and mess up our trip. You need to change your number."

"I can't."

"Why?"

"My daughter. My cell phone is my only link to her."

"When we get back, I'm going to see what I can do to help you get your daughter back. This may mean seeing Roscoe face to face."

"If it will help me get my daughter back then I think I can do it."

"You have to do it. You see he wants to intimidate you. Don't let him get to you. You have to be strong Tayla and stand up to him."

"But you don't know Roscoe."

"Make him understand that he doesn't know you as he think he does. Don't let him overpower you."

"Roscoe already knows he hold's the power."

"Then we have to take that power from him."

"If only it was that simple."

"Trust in me Tayla. It will happen."

"You don't understand Kyder."

He walked over to me and put his arms around me. "I do understand, and when we get back we'll take care of it. Relax now."

Kyder began to massage my shoulders and neck. He felt how tense I was. He knew that all hopes for Mandingo tonight had come to an end.

"Why don't we turn in," said Kyder. "We can start fresh in the morning."

"I'm sorry Kyder. I never meant to ruin our trip."

"It's not ruined. I have been having a wonderful time with you. Everything has been great. Now try not to worry. Let's turn in now."

"Okay."

Kyder didn't want me to think our trip was about getting me into bed. He thought if it happened that would be nice, but it has to happen when I'm ready.

Kyder left my room. He went into his own room and climbed into bed.

A couple of hours later I walked into his room and sat on his bed.

"Is something wrong?" he asked.

"Do you mind if I sleep in here with you? I don't want to be alone."

Kyder pulled the covers back to let me in.

I crawled into his bed.

Kyder put his arms around me and held me close. Tonight he only wanted to hold me.

I felt that Kyder was my protector, and he was protecting me from the world. I felt warm and safe in his arms, as I was drifting off to sleep.

Kyder was wide awake. He looked down into my face. He always told me he was intrigued with my beauty. He felt there was an exuberant person inside of me that was waiting to blossom. Kyder wrapped his arms tighter around me. I know my body scent was making him have a strong desire for me.

My robe opened up as he edged closer, exposing my breasts. Kyder looked on with dreamy eyes. I'm sure Mandingo was eager and hoping that this would be it.

Kyder knew that he could not make any advances no matter how Mandingo edged him on. He had to be patient and wait until I was ready. Kyder attempted to move his arm from around me. The close contact he had with me right now was agonizing for him, and Mandingo.

It was questionable if he would be able to handle lying next to me without it being a problem. It was a problem, and growing harder by the minute.

Kyder got out of bed and went outside to get some air. His body was feeling a little parched. Even though the house was fully air conditioned. He walked out on the deck and leaned against the railing. Kyder took in the cool air. To his surprise I walked out on the deck shortly after him. Apparently I couldn't sleep as well and needed some air.

"Hey you. What are you doing out here?"

"I couldn't sleep, and I didn't want to disturb you. So, I came out to get some air."

"I noticed you weren't next to me any longer. So, I came to see where you were."

I moved closer to Kyder. I took his hand in mine. "Look Kyder I don't want you to think that I'm a callous person. I'm feeling the same things that you're feeling. At first I was unsure what I was going through. I have never experienced these sensations before, but now I understand. I'm sorry if I'm sounding like a sixteen year old. My life was very isolated as a child, and with Roscoe. I never experienced a lot of things."

Kyder was getting ready to speak.

"Please, let me finish. I know that you want me, and my body is telling me that I feel the same way, but are we ready for this."

I wanted Kyder, but I was afraid of how he would feel about my inexperienced love making.

I went on. Something was coming over me.

"I wanted to release this sweltering feeling I have been experiencing."

"What are you saying Tayla?"

I utter, "I want you to show me what I have been missing all these years."

I reached up and passionately kissed Kyder. Mandingo was not going to let him turn back this time. Mandingo became auspicious, and he began to rejoice.

Kyder didn't say another word. He picked me up and carried me back to bed. Kyder gracefully laid me down and went to work.

I was a little jittery; I halted at the first touch of Mandingo. The grandiose size of him was frightening, but I stepped up. I was steadfast on giving them both what they needed, and I allowed him to have his way.

Kyder was very delicate in handling me. He could tell I was very zealous about the whole experience.

I was too excited. I rushed him on. He held me back

because he wanted it to be slow and long.

Kyder was diligent in making the feeling linger on in my mind and body. This was no ordinary experience for me. It was glorious in every way.

Once I relaxed and let the feeling enter my mind, Mandingo was easy to subdue.

I got into the rhythm of the dance with the quickness. It was a dance well done.

After the dance Kyder held me as if he was never going to let me go. I saw that he had a perplexed look on his face. I'm sure he was hoping I felt the same way he did.

From the look in my eyes he knew that I felt the same way he did. Kyder, pleased with himself held me until we drifted off to sleep.

Several days later our trip had come to an end. I was happy that I decided to accompany Kyder. The trip was everything that I had hoped it would be and more. Now, I knew it was time to face reality, face the devil about my daughter, and get back home so that I could make some money. I wasn't ready to leave just yet, but I knew what I had to do. I also had plans to check Red's out.

CHAPTER 15

Tayla

I decided it was time for me to go down and check out Red's. The little money I did have was dwindling down. It appeared that there was no hope for a regular job due to not having much experience. I needed money and I needed it fast. I didn't want Zena's place to be a long term placement for me.

Zena told me where Red's was located. I prepared myself for the ride. Zena had already left an hour ago. Thirty minutes later I left out the door to check out the show. I was hoping that I would have the nerve to dance. I needed a job and I needed it now. I didn't want to depend on Kyder. So, nerves or no nerves I knew I really didn't have any other options.

I arrived at Red's. When I walked in it was dark and I felt a little strange. I sat in a corner of the club. The show was about to start in ten minutes. A waiter came over and announced that it was a two drink minimum in the club.

I ordered a glass of wine. I wanted to be in my right mind when looking at the girls perform.

The show started and all the dancers came out and took a stroll around the club. The men began to shout and whistle as the girls danced around on the stage. Some of the men began going up to the stage and throwing dollars to them. The girls walked off then one girl after another came out. Each had their own routine as they performed.

I was looking around the club watching some of the girls who were giving table and lap dances.

Zena's turn was up. She came out and did her thing. I thought she was a wonderful dancer. The men began to go berserk as Zena put on her show. They lavished her with money. Once she finished she quickly picked up her money. She spotted me and motion for me to meet her back stage.

I got up to meet with Zena. I was pumped as I told Zena how good the show was.

"I think I can do it Zena. What do I have to do to get started?"

"Slow down for starters. Don't you think you need to check out the show a couple more times before you make a decision?"

"No, I've already made my decision.

"Tayla don't let the money hype you up. This money can be the root of all evil if you let it."

"Girl, I don't want anything but the money. I can handle this Zena. I need it."

"Tayla, I'll set up a meeting for you if you're serious about this."

"I'm very much serious. Who will I be meeting with?"

"Carlito."

"Is he here now?"

"Yes, why?"

"Let's set this up now."

"You are serious?"

"Serious as a heart attack."

"Alright. Let's do it. Come with me."

Zena led me to Carlito's office. She knocked on the door then waited for a response.

Carlito told her to come in.

"Carlito do you have a minute?"

"What's up Zena?"

"I have a friend here that's interested in taking Paula's spot. This is Tayla."

Carlito began to look me up and down. He pushed his work aside and walked around the desk where I was standing.

"Turn around," said Carlito. He was sizing me up to see what type of shape my body was in. Carlito was in the business to keep the men coming into his place of business. On some occasions women as well. In this business women and men come in to check out the show.

"Nice," said Carlito.

He was looking at my legs and butt. Have you ever stripped before?"

"Actually no, but I know I can do it"

"And what makes you think you can?"

"Well, I'm a good dancer and I have the body."

"Why now? What makes you want to get in this line of business? It can be scary out there, with all those men grabbing at you."

"Mr. Carlito as you can see. I'm a big girl. I also need the money."

"In that case, I will give you a trial run next Friday. It's up to the crowd whether I keep you on. Is that a deal?"

"Fair enough and what about the pay?"

"Three hundred a night and you keep your tips."

"That's a deal."

Carlito and I shook hands. "Thanks Mr. Carlito."

"You're very welcome. I hope I won't be disappointed."

"You won't." I said as we walked out the door.

I turned around to Zena. "Thank you Zena."

"Girl, I hope you're ready for this."

"I wouldn't be able to get out there tonight, but by Friday night I'll be ready. The time has come for me to make my own money."

"Tayla there is no hurry for you to leave my home. I told you before, you're welcome to stay as long as needed. There is no charge for you staying ay my place."

"I know Zena, and I appreciate everything you have done for me. It's time for me to learn how to stand on my own. God bless the child that's got its own."

"And what about Kyder? Do you think he'll agree with your new line of work?"

"I have no plans of telling him. I'm not planning on stripping forever. Just long enough to save some money to live on until I find a descent job."

"Well, you'll have to tell him something, if you guys get any closer. He'll wonder where you're at every night if you're not with him or he can't reach you."

"Then I'll have to keep him from getting close to me."

"Do you think that is the answer?"

"Zena, I don't know what else to do right now. I know that my goal is to make some money. I can't let anyone get in the way of that or I'll never get Kayla back. Besides, things are so complicated right now. I can't commit to Kyder or anyone else for that matter."

"Then you're doing right by taking it slow."

"My thoughts exactly."

"But don't you think your trip has made you guys a little closer?"

"Actually, closer than I ever expected. I can't let my emotions or lust get in the way of what I need to do. I like Kyder, so when the time is right I'm hoping he'll be the one in my life."

"Do you think he'll wait for you?"

"I'm hoping. Kyder is a wonderful person. Someone I would regret losing. I'm going to do as much as possible to keep him without letting him know about me stripping."

"How do you think he'll feel about you stripping?"

"The same way any other man would feel if their woman were stripping."

"Well you better hope he never finds out."

"With him working long hours at the hospital I should be okay."

"I hope so, because he is a jewel worth keeping."

"You're right. Girl that man was sho nuff good to me in Hawaii."

"Any man, besides Roscoe would be good."

"No, it's more than that. He treated me very special, and he was patient. It felt as though I was in a fairy tale. I haven't awakened yet. He keeps surprising me with new things every chance he gets."

"It seems that the good doctor is not the only one that is hooked. What did you do to him?"

"I just helped him release some long lost pressure that was overdue."

"Girl what was he holding it in for?"

"He said, "the right one."

"So, he thinks you're it."

"Seems that way. I hope I don't disappoint him."

"I'll have to teach you how to handle your business. You can have the man and make your money at the same time. You also know that Kyder has more money then you'll ever need."

"I can't depend on Kyder's money. Remember, God bless the child that's got its own. Besides, I don't want to ever be in the same boat as before. If for some reason Kyder and I don't work out, I want to have money to stand on my own."

"Well, don't be stupid and start paying bills. Bank your money and let him take care of everything else."

"I don't want to use the man. He deserves more than that."

"Girl, you'll learn."

"Enough about Kyder. Give me some advice about stripping?"

"Advice about stripping! Just get out there and do your thing. I pretend that it's just my man out there I'm dancing for. That's the only way I can get loose and relax. When I go out there I'm in a different world, and nothing else matters but pleasing him. Once that music start playing, another person comes out of me. I let the beat get me into my groove. I listen to the music and the rhythm takes me away. When I get into my routine I don't even see the men until after the music stops. So, when you get out there just think that you're dancing for Kyder, and you're getting ready to put it on him."

"Put it on him?"

"Yeah girl, throw down. Drop it like it's hot. I'm sorry. I keep forgetting your love life was jacked up, but don't worry. You have the best teacher in the world."

"Thanks, for the advice. I'll have to work on a routine before Friday."

"You don't need to work on a routine. Just get out there and let the music free your mind. Whatever you feel like doing just do it."

I needed to see if I could move like I use to. It had been some time since I last danced.

"Let's go to the club. I want to see if I still have the moves in me."

"Girl, dancing is like riding your man. Once you get started you never forget how to do it. Tomorrow I'm off. We can go then."

"That's cool Zena."

I was dressing to hit the club tonight. I had on my wide leg black pants, and back out black top.

I threw a jacket over my arms just in case the club was cool when we arrive. I remembered I always started off cool, and then once I got on the dance floor I would become hot after dancing off a few songs.

I was back to myself and I was looking finer than ever. I wasn't going to the club to pick up a man. I was going to check out the latest moves and to get my own groove back.

Zena had on a sequined top with black pants. She was excited as well to be going out to unwind. Zena thought getting out would do both of us some good. She said it would also take the stress off of her thinking about some unfinished business she has to take care of.

We arrived at a club called Resolutions. The club was bumping. The music was loud and the entire crowd was on the dance floor. Every seat was empty.

"Wow, look at this crowd," I hollered over the music.

"I see this place is hot tonight." Zena said as she bopped her head to the music.

Two guys came in after us and asked us if we wanted to dance.

Zena volunteered me. "I'm going to sit this one out. You go ahead and do your thing."

The guy grabbed me by the hand not giving me time to object.

I got on the dance floor and quickly got into my rhythm with the beat.

Zena looked surprised as she watched me. Her looked showed that she thought I had some qualities in me that have been suppressed and was waiting to come out.

I was getting down and having a good time. I danced five songs straight before I decided to take a break. The guy I was dancing with followed me back to the table. I wasn't trying to hear what he was saying. I knew I only wanted to dance and not pick up men.

Another record came on that I liked and I started moving to the beat. This time I grabbed the guy and led him to the dance floor.

Zena came on the floor and danced next to me.

"You go girl," she said. "You won't have any problems at Red's. You don't seem to be shy at all. Where did this person come from?"

"I don't know Zena. Something just came over me." I said as I danced. We danced into the wee hours of the morning. This was the first time I had a good time like this in a long time. I was happy and worry free. I danced until my feet hurt.

Friday came and it was time for me to do my thang at Red's. I had been practicing all week. I was nervous, but I still wanted to go through with it. Zena helped me pick out an outfit to wear.

We packed up our things and headed down to Red's. All the girls have to enter through a certain door. We entered the club and on our way to the dressing room we peeked out to see if it was crowed. It was dark, but not a seat was empty.

"Wow there's a lot of people out there," I said.

"What people? Remember when you get out there it's just you and Kyder."

"Yeah, you're right."

"Come on let's get dressed," said Zena. She led the way to the dressing room.

Once inside the dressing room, Zena helped me prepare for my performance.

I was getting nervous. Zena poured a shot of Patron and handed it to me to relax my nerves.

I took the glass without saying a word and gulp the shot down.

Zena said she didn't have a doubt in her mind that I would be a pro after I take that first walk.

My turn was up. I waited for my cue to walk out on my song choice of *I Wanna Sex You Up, by Color me Badd.*

My song began and I walked out. I remembered what Zena told me. I began to imagine that I was dancing for Kyder.

I was strolling, bouncing and doing my thing. The men were going wild as I performed. The music took me away as the image of Kyder came in my mind. There was money all around me on the stage. They were whistling and jumping on their feet wanting me to continue my routine. As my song ended, the men continued to throw money my way. I gathered all of my money and walked off the stage.

I was hyped. I smiled to myself as I looked at all the money they threw to me.

Carlito walked into my room. "You were great. The spot is yours if you still want it."

"Yes, I do."

"It's yours."

"Thanks Carlito."

"No problem."

I was laughing and jumping around the room.

Zena said, "Slow down girl. You know, you were really hot out there. Are you sure you haven't done this before?"

"I'm sure."

"Um hum," Zena said as she was getting ready to walk out the door. It was her time to make the men wild.

After Zena left I began to count my cash. I racked up on three hundred dollars, not including what Carlito was paying me. Tonight I was going home with more money than I had in a long time. I knew this would be my fast money to get me on my feet.

I sat back and waited for Zena to finish her second routine before we headed home. I began to think about what I had just done. I knew that stripping wasn't right, but it was a means for me at the moment. I have plans to do better and to do things differently with my life this time. I am going to take charge and control over my own life. Never again am I going to allow a man to have power over me.

CHAPTER 16

Tayla

I woke up to the sound of my phone ringing. I looked up at the clock and noticed that it was seven in the morning. I grabbed the phone and said, "Hello."

"Good morning sleepy head. I was calling to see what your plans are for tonight. Am I going to see you tonight?"

I got nervous, "Tonight?"

"Yes tonight if it's okay with you."

"Actually tonight is not a good night."

"And why is that?"

"I'm hanging out with Zena tonight. We have plans to go out with some of her friends."

"Why don't you have Zena drop you off at my house after your girl's night out?"

"I'll see what I can do. If I'm coming I'll give you a call."

"I'll see you tonight," said Kyder as he hung up the phone.

Kyder always think positive. I wondered how I was going to continue dancing and seeing him. I hung up the phone then turned over in my bed. I was tired after dancing and the shots I took last night. I had plans on resting today until it was time for me to perform tonight.

My phone ranged shortly after I dozed back off to sleep.

"Hello." There was no response.

"Hello," I said again.

"You tramp. Did you think it was over? You ain't ever going to be shit without me. You better hope you don't wake up and the ground is on top of you." Roscoe hung up the phone.

I laid in bed holding the phone in my hand. I wondered when will it all be over, and how will I end the torture Roscoe was putting me through. Something has to give I thought.

A few seconds later my phone rang again. I answered it right away.

"You're Dead," he said as he slammed the phone down in my ear.

A chill came over me. I became frightened. At this point I knew there was no hope for going back to sleep. I sat up in bed and decided to call Kyder. He always gave me strength and I felt I needed it right now. He always knew how to calm me. I dialed his cell and the call went straight to his voice mail. I left a message for him to call me back.

I got out of bed and went into the kitchen to get something to drink. I grabbed a glass and poured myself some fresh orange-carrot juice. I sat down at the table for a minute. My mind began to reflect on all the abuse I put up with Roscoe. The images became so clear in my mind. I tried to shake away the thoughts, but the pain was deeply embedded.

I closed my eyes as I attempted to hold back several watery blinks. I got up from the table and quickly decided to head to the bathroom to take a shower.

I was hoping that the warm water of the shower would ease the piercing pain in my mind of the abuse I encountered. The memory would not erase from my mind. I sat down in the shower and let the water run on me as I released my tears. I wasn't sure how long I sat in that position letting the steaming water soothe me.

As my body began to feel a sense of tranquility, I finally crawled out of the shower.

I instantly became cold and wrapped a towel around my wet body. I walked to my room and climbed into bed without drying myself off. I pulled the cover over my head and rocked myself to sleep.

An hour later Kyder was in my room taping me on the shoulder.

"Tayla, Kyder uttered," as he continuously shook me.

I lowered the cover from around my head. As Kyder looked into my eyes, he could tell that I had been crying. He grabbed for my hand and tenderly kissed it.

"What is it baby?"

"I tried to call you," I said.

"I'm sorry. I'm here now. What happened that made you like this."

Kyder was looking at my swollen, red eyes, wet hair and the fact that I climbed into bed wet.

I began to explain, "I received another call from Roscoe today. Now I'm receiving verbal threats."

"What did he say?"

"He said I'm dead."

"He's just trying to rattle you. Don't let him Tayla."

"I think whatever we try to do will make things worse."

"You have to trust me. If you don't put the law on him he will continue to harass you. He has no plans of giving Kayla up willingly. I feel it's time to call the police. You need to make a report and get a restraining order on him. You know where he works. They can serve him on the job."

"I don't know."

"This is the only way Tayla. It is not going to get

any better. It will get worse if you do nothing. You got to fight back."

"Let me think about it. Will you just hold me right now?"

Kyder climbed into bed with me. He put his arms around me and held me close. He didn't seem to care that the bed was wet from me getting in without drying myself off. I felt he just wanted to do whatever he could to make me feel better. I was glad that he was there for me. He wanted to relieve me of my pain and nothing else mattered.

We both fell asleep. It was one in the afternoon when we woke up.

"Thank you Kyder for being here for me. I just didn't know what to do."

"Don't worry. We'll figure it out together."

"Thank you again."

"For what?"

"For being in my life."

I saw something sweet and sincere in Kyder. I wished I could be exuberant about Kyder. Any women would be. I only hoped that one day I would be able to enjoy the gift that God sent me, because truly he is a blessing.

I did something I have never done before. I took the first step. I bent over and kissed Kyder. After the shock wore off he inquired in a cool voice, "Tayla what are you doing?"

"Please, just go with the flow."

The kiss was smooth and refreshing. It appeared to send a tinkling sensation to Mandingo. Today I didn't hold back. I began to undress Kyder.

He probably was thinking I needed to be tighten up the right way. The way a real man takes care of his woman. I never knew love like this before. I wondered if he tightened up on his back stroke would I develop some strength and self-confidence about myself. Kyder knew it would take more than checking out Mandingo to make me tough. He thought he would let me have my way and give me what I needed for now.

He positioned me on top of him and allowed me to take over. Kyder drove on helping me to fulfill my needs. He opened me up to a whole new world. A world full of love and lust. None like I had ever experienced before.

I was grateful and had tears in my eyes. Kyder has been wonderful to me. He had plans on helping me concerning my child and my future.

I looked into Kyder's eyes and knew that I could fall in love with him, but I had to hold back. I couldn't let that happen. Not at this point in my life.

"What is it? Asked Kyder.

I lied. "I just want to thank you for all that you have done for me."

"Tayla there is no reason to thank me. You deserve it all and more. So please stop thanking me."

I wondered if Kyder could continuously love me.

I was relaxed. I looked over at Kyder who had fallen asleep. I felt that I had slept enough for today. I eased out of bed trying not to wake him up. I decided I needed to do something with my hair before my performance tonight. As I stepped out of my room I noticed that Zena was in the kitchen.

Zena had a smile on her face from ear to ear. She didn't have to say a word. I already knew what she was thinking.

"So, the brother threw down?" said Zena.

I only smiled.

"I knew it was only a matter of time. There was no way you could be all next to that big hunk of a man without the urge to get down. A good throw down does the body and mind good."

"Yeah, I guess you're right." I sat down at the table. "Zena, I lost it this morning, and Kyder was my picker upper."

"You know it's not going to be easy. You will have your good days and your bad ones. You have been through a lot. So, when you're going through a bad day pray. Ask God to deliver you from evil."

"Why would God deliver me from evil when I'm stripping, still married and have been with another man?"

"Tayla don't you know that God is a forgiving God."

"Yes, but...."

"Girl, there is no buts with God. All you got to do is pray. He will see you through."

"You're right Zena. I know it was only him that brought me this far. I need him now, and I'm going to start back going to church. I use to go to church all the time before I met Roscoe."

"Then you should start back."

"I am, but in the mean time I'm going to do something to this nappy head of mine."

"What happen to your hair?"

"You don't want to know. So, let me get busy before Kyder wakes up and I scare him away."

"Girl, I don't think nothing is going to scare that man away from you."

I smiled. "I hope not."

"I forgot to tell you how great you were out there Tayla."

I put my finger to my lips. I didn't want Kyder to hear the conversation. "We'll talk about it later."

"Okay girl. Let me get out of your way."

I gathered all the items I needed to do my hair. I decided to complete my task in the kitchen. I turned a little boom box on low and got busy. Before I knew it I was dancing around the kitchen. I appeared to be practicing my routine for tonight's show. The sound of Kyder's voice startled me.

"If you keep dancing around in that manner, your hair will have to wait."

He grabbed me around the waist, and gave me a big hug and a savoring kiss. I let the sensation of the kiss stimulate my mind. This man was doing things to me, and it was enjoyable. Not like the pain and misery of love making with Roscoe. I was beginning to enjoy the intimacy I experienced from Kyder. I had no idea that it could be this pleasurable, and I wanted to explore more. It was all new to me, and I didn't know if I could please Kyder. I wanted to learn how to break it down and make him feel as good as he makes me feel.

I backed away from Kyder's embrace. I had to end my thoughts about him, and get myself together for tonight's show.

"Look babe. You better head out so you can get your run on, and rest for those sixteen hours you are about to do."

"I'm trying to get my run on now, if you would let me," said Kyder.

I wanted nothing more but to run and get back into the bed with Kyder, but I knew what I had to do.

"I need to do something to this fro on top of my head. It looks like a bird nest."

"Are you putting me out?"

"No, but we both have things that we need to take care of."

"Sure you're right. In that case, I guess I'll be going."

Kyder gave me another kiss and walked towards the door.

"I'll give you a call when I finish my shift," he said.

"That would be nice Kyder. Talk to you soon and please get some rest."

"Will do. Later baby."

"Okay bye."

I was relieved that Kyder was gone. I didn't know how I was going to keep up this charade. I only hoped that it would last until I was able to save up a good amount of cash. I continued on with doing my hair while listening to the radio.

I got back into my groove and began dancing around the kitchen again. I was doing my thing and began to pretend I was performing. I wanted to do something different tonight. I didn't want to use the same old boring routines night after night. My plans were to change up my acts on a regular basis.

I danced around for a good hour. Once I had my routine together I finished my hair and decided to check out what I was going to wear tonight. Then I sat down to catch my breath. As I was resting I began to think about my precious Kayla. I wondered what she was doing. I missed holding her and reading her favorite bedtime story. A tear fell from my eye. I wanted to call Roscoe. To plea with him, but I knew if I called it would be pure hell. I began to think about taking Kyder's advice.

I realized I would have to take Roscoe to court if I had any hope of ever seeing my daughter again.

Kyder had given me a little strength. I was ready to have the papers drawn up. The only place I knew I could reach him was on his job.

Roscoe worked at the Post Office. I knew the location and the hours he worked. I also knew I would be placing myself in more danger if I served him papers on his job. He left me no other choice. It was eating me up not seeing my daughter or even knowing where she is.

I was ready to stand up and fight. I saw no other way. I made a mental note to inform Kyder to help me with doing whatever I needed to do to file the papers.

***

Zena and I left for Red's at nine o'clock. Once we arrived we went straight to our dressing room. Tonight we didn't peep at the crowd. The nervousness I had had worn off. I was ready because now I had another goal in mind. I knew I would have to pay a lawyer to help get Kayla back. So now, I had to save more money.

I knew I had to get on that stage and make the crowd love me. I needed the money more than ever now.

The time came for me to do my first routine. I walked out on the stage with grace and confidence. My demeanor said this is my night. I wore a glittery bright red teddy that was trimmed in costume diamonds. The crowd was going wild the minute I stepped out on stage. The men were whistling and throwing money right away. I ambled over to the pole and did my pole dance.

The men were all up on their feet. The security guards had to hold two men back who attempted to run on the stage. They were escorted out of the club.

The action that was going on had no effect on me. I continued my routine as if the mob that was trying to get to me wasn't there.

There was so much money on the stage that I was dancing on top of it.

Once my routine was over I could barely pick up all the money.

Carlito came to my room and taped on the door.

"Wow, what a show. I'm not sure if you should go out again tonight."

"But, I have to. I need the money."

"Look I have a proposition for you."

"Wait Carlito, I'm not into the extra stuff here. I just want to dance."

Carlito held a business card up between his fingers. "This may be worth your while. He only wants your company, and he's willing to give you a thousand dollars just for sitting with him, and nothing more."

"You mean. This man wants to give me a thousand dollars just to listen to him talk?"

"Yes"

"Unbelievable."

"Tayla, it happens all the time."

"I don't know Carlito."

"Well, here is his card. You make the decision."

I couldn't believe it. Someone wanted to pay me to spend time with him, and nothing sexual. It was too good to be true I thought.

Zena walked into the dressing room. I had just finished my routine.

"Dang girl, I heard you were raw."

"Look Zena. Carlito just handed me this card. A Mr. Zindale wants to pay me a thousand dollars just to sit with him. Could this be true?"

"Yes Tayla. Mr. Zindale is a rich and lonely man. He got so much money, and he comes to the club all the time and help out the girls. He knows they must need money or they wouldn't be stripping. So he gives it out freely all the time. He is paralyzed from the waist down. He was in a bad accident. He won't be a problem. He likes talking and looking at beautiful women. It's definitely worth the time."

"Girl, if that's all I got to do is listen to him, then I think I can do that."

"If he's calling on you, then go for it."

"When should I let him know?"

"Right now girl. Don't waste time or he'll choose another girl."

I wanted to listen to what Zena was saying. I wanted to see him before I actually went out there with him.

"Zena, which one is he?"

"Come on," said Zena. "I'll show you. You can't miss him. He was something else until he had that accident."

"What do you mean something else?"

"You know a brother was packing. He was very built in all the right places. It's a shame that all of that has gone to waste."

Zena and I peeped through the curtains.

"Over there."

Zena pointed to a nice looking man. He was dressed very nicely. You could see that he was sitting in a wheelchair.

"Okay," I said. "I want to do it."

"I'm sure he's waiting for you if Carlito gave you his card."

"Then I won't keep him waiting any longer."

I walked out and went over to Mr. Zindale's table.

"Hello."

"Hello. You were great out there."

"Thank you."

"Please have a seat. Would you like something to drink?"

"A glass of wine would be nice."

Mr. Zindale ordered a glass of wine for me and a drink for himself. He began talking about his life and his accident. There was nothing for me to say.

I thought he really must be lonely with no one to talk to. I also wondered how a man that rich could be lonely. He could get a million women to listen to him. Why would he want strippers to listen to him talk?

I wanted to find out. I wanted to know more about Mr. Zindale.

CHAPTER 17

Tayla

Sunday came and I got up early and prepared myself for church. I needed to hear the word today. I also wanted to be in the house of the Lord when I put my prayer in today. I ate my breakfast and hurried out the door. I wanted to arrive early before the congregation started to roll in. I had plans of going to the altar about my problems. I wanted to bend down on my knees and pray to God to deliver me from this madness, and to watch over Kayla, and return her safely.

I arrived at the church, and as I hoped no one was in the sanctuary. I walked in and went straight to the altar. I bent down on my knees, closed my eyes and begun to pray.

I prayed for forgiveness for stripping and for all of my sins in my life. I prayed for Zena, world peace, for Kayla, a better job, and asked God to enlarge my territory. I also prayed for a peace of mind. Before I finished praying a man walked into the sanctuary and up to the altar. He had no idea that I was there because I was on bended knees.

I heard someone approaching and quickly stood up.

He said, "I'm sorry I didn't mean to interrupt you."

I wiped the tears from my eyes before saying, "I was finished."

He was very observant. He told me there was something heavy in my eyes, and he was a counselor at the church and at a hospital. So, I'm sure he knows the signs.

"Are you new here at First Baptist Church?"

"I'm not a member, but I've been here several times."

"Well, I'm Jordan, and welcome."

"I'm Tayla Anderson."

"Nice to meet you Sister Anderson. Will you be staying for the service?"

"Yes, I will."

"Great. I would love to talk with you more after the service. If it's okay with you."

I think that he thought I needed a word of encouragement. Maybe he felt and saw it in my face that I was going through something.

"Sure, I'll see you after service."

Several members started to flow in. I walked off to grab a seat. More and more members began to arrive and the congregation was quickly filling up the church.

Jordan found his seat in the sanctuary as the music from the organ, drums and piano sounded out an old doctor watts song. The church was called to worship.

Everyone started singing until one of the deacons began to pray. Then the morning hymn *Woke up this morning with my mind on Jesus was sung.* A minister and the congregation followed with a responsive reading from the book of Psalms.

Everyone was standing when the morning prayer began as the choir led. Then the announcements of the church were read, and the choir sang my favorite song, *Be Blessed.*

I was touched by the song. Various members from the choir and congregation sang solo then passed the mike. Everyone was up on their feet including me praising God. Tears began to flow from my eyes. I knew even though I was going through hard times, living without my precious Kayla and suffered the loss of a child, I'm still blessed.

I knew it wasn't anybody but God seeing me through.

The ushers passed the tray for tithes and offerings, after the choir completed several selections. It was now time for the message. I needed to hear the Word. I enjoyed listening to the minister of the church speak. I would bring my note pad whenever I come to church to take notes on what the minister preached about. From time to time I would look over my notes whenever I needed a spiritual uplifting.

I knew I wasn't saved as I should be, but I was asking God to work on me to be a better Christian. As the minister said, I didn't want to be a lukewarm Christian.

Today the minister was very powerful. He stated, "Whatever you are going through, be strong, It's only a test. You have to learn how to be patient in your pain, and wait on God, and sometimes you have to go through a whole lot before the Lord shows up."

The minister went on to say, "It's dangerous to be dead on your feet." This means you're not trying to do better or move forward. You're dead or stuck in the same position.

He said, "The Word of God will change your life. The Lord sends us through things to see if we will remain faithful. God is trying to build you up to bring out what he has placed on the inside of you. Let go and let God. You can't change the past, but you can change your attitude. You got to pray when dealing with evil. The devil will wear you down to do all he can to discourage you, but God wants to tell you to be encouraged."

I felt that this service was for me. I thought the minister was talking to me. I got what I needed today as I was filled with the Word and I felt empowered. I made up in my mind that I would start coming to church on a regular basis. I needed to be here and I planned on coming every Sunday.

After church was over I waited around for a minute. I didn't know why I was waiting, but something held me here.

Several members of the church stopped to talk to Jordan. He tried to get away, but someone was always stopping him.

I noticed how busy he was and decided to leave. I began heading for the door when he caught up to me. He asked me if we could talk in the office.

I followed him to the office. He closed the door for privacy. Once I entered Jordan turned around to face me.

"Would you like to have a seat?"

"Sure Jordan."

"Sister Anderson, tell me if I'm wrong. I noticed that your

heart is heavy when you were at the altar. Is there something I can help you with? I'm a counselor here at the church. I would like to talk with you some time. My services to you would be free of charge. Think of it as one Christian to another."

I was still in church, so I knew I shouldn't lie. Something kept me after church. I wondered if it was God trying to get me some help.

I began telling Jordan my story. It all came out so easy about Roscoe, and the abuse.

Jordan listened and took a few notes.

I finished talking, and Jordan said, "Let me see if I understand what you said." He summed up my story and hit everything right on the head.

Jordan said, "I can see that you truly need some help. I'm here to tell you that you've come to the right place. You do understand that you need to work on getting yourself together before you can even concentrate on your daughter. Now, let's set up an appointment for next week. What day is good for you?"

I thought that I would try the counseling. It couldn't hurt I thought. "Thursday's are good for me."

"Great. Let's say about 6 p.m."

"Six it is."

"You take care of yourself and I'll see you on Thursday."

"Thank you, Jordan."

"No, it's my pleasure. Let me walk you out."

"Jordan, would you mind saying a prayer with me before I

leave?"

"Not a problem."

Jordan held my hands and said a prayer for me.

***

I drove home with a smile on my face. For the moment I felt equipped to make it through the day. All I could do was take it one day at a time.

I headed home with nothing else in mind to do, but to get something to eat. I felt like cooking a spread today. I use to cook a big Sunday dinner like my mother and grandmother use to cook.

I turned my car around after thinking about my dinner, and I headed down to the grocery store.

Once inside I picked out a roast, potatoes, carrots, and greens, the ingredients for some homemade macaroni and cheese, and corn bread. I paid for my purchase and headed home for a second time.

I made it home and took my groceries inside. I changed into something a little more comfortable then started cooking my meal.

Zena came out of her room when she smelled the aroma of the food.

"I thought I smelled the sweet aroma of something cooking, and heard pots and pans clicking."

"And you were right. I felt like cooking today."

"That's good. Is Kyder coming over today?"

"No, he's working a double. I won't see him for a couple of days."

"Then he's missing a treat."

"I can always cook for him later."

"I'm sure he would enjoy that," said Zena.

Zena began to look into the pots.

"What are you cooking?"

I told her about the meal I was cooking.

"Ain't nothing like some good old soul food."

"I agree."

We both laughed.

"Let me get out of your way. I'm looking forward to this meal. I have to make a run. I'll be back in a few."

"Okay."

Zena left and I went back to stirring my pots, and adding more seasoning. I was doing my thing in the kitchen. I had become accustom to turning on the music whenever I was doing things around the house.

Today, I turned the radio on to a church station. As I was cooking I prayed to God again to ask for forgiveness of my sin. I felt bad about stripping, but I saw no other way at this time.

I continued on with my chore at hand until my dinner was

done. I sat down and decided to relax and watch a Sunday movie on TV. I was flipping through the channels to find a movie when my cell phone ranged.

"Hello."

"You better get your freaking ass home."

"Home Roscoe, where would that be?"

"What the hell you mean where would that be? You stupid slut. You have always been dumb. I don't know why I married you."

I was very calm. "Me either," I spit out. "Why did you marry me Roscoe?"

"You were convenient at the time. I never loved you. Do you think I could love someone like you?"

I ignored his question. "Look Roscoe. It doesn't have to be like this, but I refuse to let you continue to abuse me."

"Abuse you. Girl, I haven't done a damn thing to you. If I did do something that you call abuse, you must have done something to make it happen."

"No Roscoe."

"Tayla, you're causing me a lot of problems, and my time."

"Your time, what do you mean?"

"You know I don't have time to keep a whining child."

I wanted to cry at this point when I heard that my child has been crying. I refused to let Roscoe see me weak.

"Did you ever think that maybe she needs her mother."

"As far as I'm concerned her mother is dead."

I didn't respond. Roscoe was surprised that I wasn't crying and pleading for him to give Kayla back. He snapped.

"Who the hell you been sleeping with? Some man got your stupid ass head."

"No Roscoe, I just finally woke up."

"Someone has been talking to you. You're too stupid to make any decisions on your own. Dumb ass."

Click. I hung up the phone.

"No the hell she didn't hang up on me." Roscoe was furious. I'm sure he felt he could strangle me if he was next to me. He tried to call my number back. There was no answer.

I refused to answer the call.

I know Roscoe was mad when I hung up on him. I could picture him throwing the phone up against the wall.

CHAPTER 18

Tayla

I was having my first session with Jordan. I arrived at the church fifteen minutes early. I wanted to put in a prayer at the altar before I met with him.

I knew I had a lot of things to talk to God about and a lot of forgiveness I needed to pray for.

I walked into the sanctuary and looked around. I was happy that no one was here. I walked to the altar and bent down on my knees. I began to Thank God for all that he had done for me. I prayed for the safe return of Kayla, a job to be able to care for my daughter and happiness. I also asked God to forgive me for all of my sins. Jordan walked out of the office as I was asking God to put my prayer in his will and let his will be done.

"Tayla, I'm glad you made it."

"Yes, me too. I was undecided about coming."

"Well, let's go into the office and get started now that you're here."

I followed Jordan into the office. Once I walked in, he closed the door behind me.

Jordan tried to break the ice with small talk to get me to relax. He talked about his position at the church as a counselor. He even told me a joke that made me laugh. Then he eased in "What brings you to the altar?" I began to get comfortable enough to talk with Jordan.

I talked about my abuse with Roscoe, losing my child and about Kayla.

Jordan asked me to go back in time in order for him to get some history about my life. He inquired about my childhood and my parents. As I talked, Jordan jotted down some notes. He allowed me to talk then asked me a few questions.

Jordan gave me a few suggestions. For today, I felt a little relieved with getting it all off my chest.

Jordan and I met several more times after my first session. Some of the sessions were at the church, away from the church and even at my home. We would take walks together in the park, down to the pier, and even at the race track. We would never bet on the horses, but it was relaxing standing at the rails as the wind blowed in my hair while watching the horses' race. The atmosphere was therapeutic and it gave me a peace of mind.

I believed that Jordan knew, as I did, that our time together was helping me. I suppose he was enjoying my company as well. We had been meeting for six months once a week.

I also sensed Jordan was starting to feel a connection with me. I could tell by him calling me so much and I could hear it in his voice. I think the time we began to spend together was making him want to get closer to me. His questions were telling me that he wanted to know more about me personally. He also wanted to help get some of the stress off of me. The way he looked at me made me feel that he thought there was something intriguing about me. I sensed he wanted to be with me to relieve me of all my worries and problems. But there was one problem. He was married, and has been for twelve years. Besides, I'm not looking to get involved with anyone at this time. Now I feel Jordan wants to move from counselor to lover with me.

I began asking him questions. I wanted to know a little about his life because I was telling him everything about me. Jordan seemed a little skeptical about revealing his true feeling about his life. I wondered why he was holding back. I wondered if it was because he knew what he was feeling was not right.

We began meeting more often and today, Jordan had big plans for us he said.

Today we were going to meet at Brazzaz's, a nice Brazilian Restaurant. Jordan said he wanted to provide me with a nice meal, and then take me for a walk so we could really talk in private. He appeared excited over the mere fact that he would be seeing me today. Jordan knew that I wanted to know more about his life. He had told me a few things. So maybe he was going to open up to me tonight. I had a few questions of my own about him that I needed answering.

Jordan gave me a little information about his life. His wife's name is Candice. They have three children, two boys who are not by him, and one girl, Justine they have together. She is in high school. Some of their problems were due to one of the boys. I could tell he needed someone to talk to as I did.

One session Jordan told me he understands when I said Roscoe and I had problems connecting and we didn't feel close to each other for a long time. I felted this must be part of his problem as well. Jordan told me that that he felt his wife wasn't a good communicator. He said she would hold everything inside and refuse to talk about whatever was bothering her until she was ready to explode. He stated his wife revealed that she felt she was in the marriage alone, and he was not putting in his share at home, and with her.

Jordan said he would be exhausted after putting in all those hours. So, when he came home he would eat and go to bed. He mentioned that he tried to explain this to Candice, but the explanation wasn't good enough to her. Jordan said she would continuously let him know that she needed more help at home, but no change took place. Jordan said Candice was complaining all the time, and their sex life was only once or twice a month which added to the long list of their problems.

I think that even though Jordan was a counselor he was unable to work on his own problems at home. He was so busy helping other people that he didn't take the time to save his own marriage. Jordan said his wife was constantly asking him to participate more in the marriage, but he didn't feel connected to her any longer so he just gave up and wouldn't try. He said he felt they had grown apart and now they were sleeping in separate bedrooms. So getting things together was the furthest thing from his mind at this time.

I began to think that I was occupying so much of his mind time that it was getting harder for him to meet with me for the sessions. It seemed as though he wanted to talk to me every moment that he had. Some days I think he would call me just to hear my voice. He really wouldn't have much to say during some of those calls. I know he must be wondering if I could feel the attraction he was throwing off. Boy, it seems as though my mind is on him as well. Let me snap out of this trance about Jordan.

Jordan told me he would arrive at the restaurant before me. I'm sure he wanted to be sitting at the table just to watch me walk in.

I arrived shortly after Jordan was seated at the table. I walked in and his eyes lit up as if an angel had walked through the door.

Jordan sat up with excitement as he watched me walk towards him.

The atmosphere of the restaurant was nice and warm, with dim lights. As I was walking towards him I could almost read his mind. I saw him envisioning my face in his mind and his heart began to flutter. I'm sure he has tried to stop the feelings he was experiencing, but he didn't have any control over them. Jordan's facial expression exposed his mind. His expression showed me that he wished he could have me and he was hoping it could be for more than just one night.

Jordan's face continued to sparkle with excitement as he watched me walk towards him. The atmosphere of the restaurant gave me a cozy feeling.

"Hello."

"Hi," Jordan said as he stood up and pulled out a chair for me.

"Have you been waiting long?" I asked.

"No, only for a few minutes."

"Good."

"Would you like something to drink," asked Jordan.

"A glass of wine would be nice."

Jordan ordered our drinks. He appeared to be a little nervous. I wondered did he need the drink to lighten up this mood. Jordan also appeared to have something on his mind.

"How was your day today?" he asked.

"I'm good, but miss my baby so much."

"I understand. You still haven't heard from Kayla?"

"No, but someone keep calling my phone and hanging up. I know its Roscoe. He gets a kick out of taunting me."

"Then don't let him. You have to show him that he doesn't control you any longer."

"That would only make him madder."

"Either way, he's going to be mad. No matter what you say or do."

"Yeah, I guess you're right."

The waiter brought over our drinks.

"Look, I have something I would like to talk to you about."

"Go ahead. I'm all ears."

Jordan took a sip of his drink as he prepared to spit out what he wanted to say.

"Tayla we have been spending a lot of time together and I feel that I have really become close to you. I don't make it a practice to get close to the people that I counsel, but for some reason I can't seem to stop thinking about you."

"Jordan."

"No, let me finish. I know that you are going through something right now, but I want you to know that I'm here for you."

Jordan cleared his throat before he continued.

"I want more than a counselor relationship."

I wasn't surprised but I found it flattering. Before now men wouldn't even look my way, now I have two men trying to get with me. Who would have ever imagined that I would have to make a choice between two handsome and wonderful men. I thought Jordan was handsome and I was beginning to feel something for him as well, but I wasn't sure what it was. So I kept it to myself. I knew I would never act on my feelings. I wasn't the type of person that would take the first step with a man, besides I was already dealing with Kyder. I never considered myself as a player, nor had more than one man at a time. I didn't know if I could handle both of them.

I thought about it for a moment. Kyder had money and he wanted to take care of me. I believe he would make a very good provider. If I would just allow him, but I wouldn't let him. I was too independent for that. Besides money never impressed me, but it helps. It's the small things that really matter to me most. Kyder really knows how to treat a woman. I just hope it continues and he doesn't change. Men do many things to get you, but they don't continue it or maintain it to keep you.

I thought again about Jordan. I felt a connection with him. I thought maybe it was because he was learning about me inside and out. He had learned my whole life story. As a counselor

Jordan knew everything about me. Down to the littlest things like what makes me happy and what makes me sad. On top of it all we were spending a lot of time together. The real question is how is he in bed, I thought?

I shook my head, wondering if it was the wine that was making me think this way. I was in deep thought.

"Hey," said Jordan.

"I'm sorry. I seemed to have spaced out for a minute."

"I hope what I said doesn't make you feel differently about me or uncomfortable."

"Oh no Jordan, I'm cool. Actually I'm flattered."

"So, what I said doesn't bother you?"

"No, Jordan. I'm a big girl. I'm learning how to deal with things better now. What you said doesn't bother or frighten me at all. There was a time when I wouldn't have known how to handle what you said, but my life is changing for the better now."

"Let's talk about you for once. Tell me what has been going on in your life?" I asked.

Jordan finally opened up more and told me the whole story about him and Candice. He said he wanted to leave but didn't want to hurt her.

Jordan had a lot going on in his life. I'm not sure if he can fix his own problem. I asked Jordan, "Why do you want to get involved with me?"

He said, "I really can't explain it. It's something about you that I'm attracted to. I don't want to give you any false hope, so let me lay the cards on the table. I don't know what I'm expecting to get out of being with you. I don't know what would happen if we get involved. We will just have to take it one day at a time."

"What about your marriage?"

"My marriage has been over a long time ago. Right now I'm just hanging in there for the kids and until Candice can do better by herself."

"I don't know. Let me think about all of this."

"I know it's asking a lot of you to deal with a man that's married."

I wondered if I should tell him about Kyder. "Look Jordan, I'm already in a relationship with someone, and I'm not ready to give him up either."

"I'm not in a position to ask you to give him up. All I'm saying is that I want to spend some time with you."

"I don't know. I have never done something like this before."

"I'll tell you what. Let's take it one day at a time. I would like to be friends, and if something more develops out of this, then we'll decide then. Is that a deal?"

"I still need time to think about this before I make any decisions."

"That's fair."

I'm sure Jordan wanted more, but he had no other choice. He had to do it my way. I could sense that he would be doing everything in his power to make me fall in love with him.

I was impressed by the restaurant. Many different waiters were bringing out food to our table. The Brazilian Steakhouse was wonderful. The surroundings were elegant. You are given a chip that you keep face up on the table. When you had enough food you turn the chip over and the waiters will not come to your table. They were bringing out Filet Mignon, Top Sirloin, Rack of Lamb, Bottom Sirloin, Beef Ribs, Pork Ribs, Garlic Beef Coulette, New York Strip, Pork Tenderloin, Black Pepper Filet Mignon, Bacon Filet Mignon, Chicken, Bacon Chicken Breast, and Shrimp. They also had a wonderful salad bar.

Jordan and I tried a little bit of every type of meat they had. I was so full that I could hardly walk to my car. I thanked Jordan for the evening.

"Would it be okay if I called you sometimes?"

"That would be nice, Jordan."

Jordan gave me a hug, and then closed my car door once I got inside.

"I'll talk to you soon," he said.

As I drove home I began to think how Kyder was so busy at work that we didn't even have time to spend together. This left the door open for another man to win my heart.

Chapter 19

Zena

I finally was having an outing with Roscoe and Kayla today. I was getting the chance to meet Ms. Kayla. I knew that no sex would be involved due to Kayla being present. So today, I would have to really win Roscoe over with his daughter. I knew that I had to make Roscoe trust me. That would be the only way that he would be willing to leave Kayla with me. I also knew that it would take some time to get him to that point.

I was meeting them at Chucky Cheese. This wasn't one of my favorite places to attend, but I knew the reason I had to go.

Roscoe and Kayla were already there when I arrived. I saw Roscoe watching Kayla as she climbed through the tunnels and slided down into the balls. I walked over to Roscoe and gave him a hug.

Roscoe hugged me back as he kept his eyes on Kayla. He

was relieved that she wasn't watching. Roscoe pointed towards Kayla as she played.

"God I miss you," said Roscoe.

"I know. I miss you too. It seems as though it's been so long."

"It has been too long. I have been so busy working and taking care of Kayla that I haven't had time for anything else."

I played the game. "Have you heard from her mother?"

"No, she hasn't called. She just abandoned her child. I don't care about her leaving me, but her own child. No mother in their right mind would leave their child.

I wanted to say the kind that was being abused. I held my tongue, not wanting Roscoe to get suspicious.

Roscoe looked up to see Kayla running towards us.

"Here she comes," he said.

"Kayla this is Zena. She is a friend of daddy."

"Hi Kayla, it's good to meet you," I said as I held out my hand to shake Kayla's hand.

Kayla only looked. Roscoe told her to go ahead and shake Ms. Zena's hand.

"Zena is good enough for me. Kayla doesn't have to call me Ms. Zena."

I held my hand out again and this time Kayla shook my hand.

"You're such a pretty girl Kayla," I said.

Kayla only looked. She didn't say a word.

"Tell Zena, thank you Kayla," said Roscoe.

"Daddy what am I saying thank you for?" asked Kayla.

"Well, anytime someone gives you a compliment you should tell them thank you."

"What's a commit?"

"It's a compliment. You should say thank you whenever someone says something nice about you. Like Zena said you are pretty."

"Oh, thank you."

"You're welcome. Would you like to play some of the games Kayla?"

"Yes. I like this one."

Kayla pointed to a game where you hit the head of monkeys when they pop up. You get tickets each time you hit their head, and depending on the number of tickets you receive you can select a prize.

I let Kayla lead the way to the game that she wanted to play. Roscoe followed behind us.

We played several games with Kayla. Then she decided that she wanted to get back into the balls.

Roscoe was trying to set up a date with me as Kayla played in the balls.

I knew that it was no way that I could say no. I had to continue with the plan now that I met Kayla. I had to win Roscoe trust and then I was going to take Kayla to be with her mother.

"Okay Roscoe, when do you want to get together?"

"Tomorrow I can meet you at our spot." He was speaking of the hotel we always meet at.

"You set everything up with the room and I'll be there to check in," I said. I wanted Roscoe to spend his money.

"Good, Consider it done. I'll make the arrangements."

Roscoe order a pizza and drinks, but Kayla was so tired that she was falling asleep as she sat at the table.

"I think it's time for me to take Kayla home."

"Your right, 'cause she has played herself out."

"Let me get her home, and I'll talk to you later."

"Okay, Roscoe."

***

The next day I arrived at the hotel and checked in. I wanted to have time to unwind before Roscoe arrived. My normal routine was to take a nice, hot bubbling bath and drink a glass of wine. Then I would slip into something a little more comfortable, and wait for his arrival.

Today, Roscoe was late. I arrived at three for check in. Roscoe finally walked in an hour and a half late at four-thirty.

Roscoe came in apologizing about being late. "I'm sorry. Kayla didn't want me to leave. She goes through those spells when she doesn't want me to leave her."

"I understand Roscoe. No need to apologize. I know how children can be. Why don't you go and take your shower and I'll fix you a drink. You seem as though you need to unwind."

"You're right. Being a Father and Mother is hard work."

"Yeah, it can be a little tough."

"Here baby," I said as I passed Roscoe his drink. I wanted to get him tipsy, so that he would agree to let me spend some time with Kayla alone.

"Why don't you take a seat, and let me run your bath water. I want to give you a bath." I said as I took my tongue and traced the lining of his lips.

Roscoe sat down as he was instructed. He began taking off his shoes, and his clothing. I went into the bathroom and ran him a nice warm bath. I had some chamomile tea in a plug in coffee cup that I was keeping warm. I poured the tea into Roscoe bath water. The tea would help him to relax along with his drink.

I led Roscoe into the bathroom once his bath water was complete. I guided him into the tub as he held onto his drink. I took the soap and lathered up the towel. I began to wash Roscoe up in a slow seductive motion. I didn't know if it was the drink or what was making him feel so relaxed and wanting. He wanted me and his manhood was getting harder by the minute. I knew he wanted me, but I wanted to make him wait this time. I continued to wash his body, and I inched closer and closer to his manhood. I washed his inner thighs as I looked into his eyes.

Roscoe looked around for somewhere to lay his glass.

"What is it baby?" I asked.

"Can you take this glass for me?" he asked.

"Why don't you finish your drink?" I didn't want his hands to be free. I knew if his hands were free he would be reaching for me and I would not be able to stop him.

On purpose I touched him in spots and places that I knew would have an effect on him. I knew how to stir him up.

After I felt Roscoe had enough, I asked him to get out of the tub. Once he got out, I began to dry him off. Roscoe loved the treatment that he was receiving from me.

I gave him the towel to continue drying himself off and went into the other room to wait for him.

Roscoe came out after five minutes. He was relaxed and his eyes showed that he had only one thing on his mind. His expression showed he wanted to lay it down on me. It had been a while since he had been with me and he needed to release the built up pressure inside of him.

Roscoe fixed himself another drink then turned on the radio. He found a smooth R & B radio station. He held out his hand and asked me to dance with him. We slow danced to *Your Body, by Slique.* Roscoe loved that song. That was all that I needed. I took it from there. I pushed Roscoe on the bed and began to do a private dance for him. He hadn't seen me dance in a long time. I twirled, bounced, and bent down like I was doing a pole dance. I put everything I had into the dance. Roscoe looked on like he could eat me up. I saw the look in his eyes, and knew he wanted me so bad. I kept on performing.

Finally I gave in and gave Roscoe what he wanted. Roscoe grabbed me and just held me in his arms. He didn't want to let me go.

"What's up Rocky?" I asked.

"I just want to hold you, and enjoy this moment."

I was hoping that this man was not getting caught up. I know he's crazy, and his emotions are going to be tripping very hard.

"Look babe. I wanted to tell you that I really enjoyed spending time with you and Kayla. When can we do it again?"

"I don't know, but soon."

"I was thinking that maybe we can take Kayla to the movies or the park, and out to eat this weekend."

"This weekend?"

"Yes why not."

"We'll see."

"Come on baby. If you don't want to go, then let me take Kayla. I'll be glad to take her and you can get some rest."

"I'm not sure that she will go with you. She doesn't take well to other people."

"I'm sure I'll be able to convince her to come with me. I'll tell her that I will take her to McDonald's or something."

"Let's see if she goes with you willingly. I don't mind, but if she starts to cry I won't make her go."

"Okay, we'll see how she takes it."

"Now, let's get some rest before we leave."

On Saturday Roscoe and Kayla met me at the Park. We allowed Kayla to play in the playground area for awhile. I pushed Kayla while she was on the swings, and then took her over to the sliding board to let her slide down. We were having so much fun together. Kayla was opening up to me.

I told Roscoe that he could go ahead and leave and I would call him to find out where to drop Kayla off.

Roscoe was reluctant to leave at first. I pushed him off, and told him to go ahead. "Kayla will be fine. See, she is feeling comfortable around me already. Trust me. I will take care of her and bring her home soon."

Roscoe told Kayla he was leaving and I would be dropping her off later. Kayla didn't care about him leaving as long as she didn't have to go.

"Okay daddy, bye."

Roscoe was shocked. He just knew that Kayla was not going to be happy if he left her. He walked away, checking behind him several times. Kayla was laughing and playing with me. She was having such a good time. Roscoe hadn't seen her happy in a long time. He left and went home to get some rest.

Thirty minutes after Roscoe left. I got on the phone and tried to call Tayla. I was so nervous that I could barely dial the number. Her phone just continued to ring.

"Damn Tayla, where are you?" The call went to her voice mail. I left her a message and told her to call right away. It's very important I said, before hanging up the line.

Tayla called back several minutes later. "Zena, is everything okay? You sound as if something is wrong."

"Tayla, are you sitting down?"

"Why?"

"Girl, you are not going to believe this."

"Believe what Zena?"

"Tayla please don't faint when I tell you."

"Zena, tell me what?"

"I'm with Kayla."

"Stop playing Zena. That's not funny."

"I'm not playing, listen."

I gave the phone to Kayla. "Speak to your mother sweetie."

"Mommy," Kayla yelled into the phone.

I heard Tayla say, "Oh my God! Kayla. How are you doing?" she began to cry.

"Mommy, Mommy, please don't cry."

"I'm sorry Kayla. It's just that Mommy misses you."

"Mommy I want to come with you."

"I know sweetie. Mommy wants you to come with me to. Where is your daddy?"

"He left, and Zena is taking me home after we leave the park."

"Let me talk to Zena."

"Okay Mommy. Please come and pick me up."

"I'll try baby. I'm working on it now."

Kayla passed the phone back to me.

"Look Tayla, I'll explain everything later. I'm going to bring Kayla home to you."

Tayla was sobbing loudly now. I know that she couldn't believe that this was happening.

"Okay Zena, I'll be waiting," she said as she hung up the phone.

I told Kayla that we were going home. I took Kayla by the hand and led her to the car.

"Kayla, do you want to see your mother?"

"Yes Zena."

"Okay, then let's go."

I drove home very nervously. I kept looking over my shoulder hoping Roscoe was not trailing me. I even checked my cell phone several times making sure that he wasn't calling. So far everything was good.

I was pulling up into my drive way twenty minutes later. Tayla was outside pulling at the door before I could park the car.

She grabbed Kayla out of the back seat and ran into the house with her. She held her and wept saying Thank You God. I can't believe that I'm finally with my child again.

I walked into the house and closed the door.

"Thank you Zena. How did you do it?"

"Tayla it's not over yet. I know that Roscoe is going to be calling in a few minutes when I don't show up with Kayla."

"Does he know where you live Zena?"

"No he doesn't, but he has my cell phone number."

"You can change your cell phone number?"

The sound of my phone ringing made us jump.
I looked at my phone and said, "It's Roscoe."

"Are you going to answer it?"

"I have to tell him something."

"So what are you going to tell him?"

"I'm going to tell him the truth. That Kayla is with her mother."

"He's going to go crazy. You don't know what you have just done."

"Tayla trust me. I do know. I did this for you. Please don't question what I've done. If it's going to be a problem I can tell Roscoe that I'm bringing Kayla back."

"I'll never let her go back to him."

"Are you sure this is what you want? You know Roscoe is going to go crazy as hell."

"Well, he doesn't know where you live. That's on my side, and now I'm ready to get a restraining order on him."

"Now you're thinking."

My phone continued to ring. I looked at it and noticed that Roscoe was still calling. I took a deep breath before answering the call.

"Hey, where are you guys? I have been waiting for your call."

"Roscoe, Kayla won't be coming home. I took her to be with her mother."

"What are you talking about?"

"I repeated myself. Kayla is with her mother."

"Zena, don't play with me. I know damn well that you don't know her mother." Roscoe was screaming in the phone. Why are you playing these games?"

"No Roscoe that's what you were doing. The games are over. I do know Tayla. In fact she's right her with me."

I handed the phone over to Tayla. "Here speak to him."

Tayla acted afraid. She didn't want to hear his voice. She knew the conversation was not going to be nice.

"Hello Roscoe. Kayla is here with me."

Before she could finish her sentence Roscoe snapped.

"You Bitches. You better bring my daughter back to me if you know what's good for you two."

"I'm sorry Roscoe. That's not going to happen. Kayla will be staying with me. You need to understand that."

"You understand this. Your ass is dead once I get a hold of you."

Tayla hung up the phone.

Chapter 20

Tayla

I was meeting Jordan at a school today. I arrived there before him and parked my car. Shortly after I arrived I called him on his cell phone to see how far he was away.

"Hey, where are you?"

"I'm ten minutes away. I'm waiting for the train to pass. Are you there yet?"

"Yes."

"I'll be there shortly."

"Okay."

I sat in my car and waited for Jordan to pull up. I turned on a CD that I made, and listened to my favorite CD of slow songs. I looked up and Jordan was pulling into the parking lot.

He parked his car, got out and walked around to the passenger side of my car.

"Hello."

"Hey you," I said.

"How was your day today?" he asked.

"Today was fine, but let me tell you what happened yesterday?"

"Go ahead."

Excitedly I said, "My daughter was returned back to me."

"You mean Roscoe gave her back to you?"

"Actually no, Somehow Zena brought her home to me."

"Zena?"

"Yes. She called me on the phone and told me to sit down. I'm here with Kayla she said. I thought she was playing a sick game or something. I couldn't believe it, but it was true."

"That's wonderful. So, Roscoe gave her to Zena to bring to you?"

"No! Somehow Zena was able to get her from Roscoe. I don't know all the details. I don't care as long as I have my daughter."

I could tell Jordan wondered how Zena got involved. He didn't want to push the issue. He kept quiet to hear what part Zena played in all of this.

"I'm glad for you Tayla. I told you all you had to do was have a little faith."

"And you were right, but you know sometimes it get hard having faith when you are going through changes in your life."

"No matter what Tayla, you can never doubt God. Place your problems in his hands. Trust me. God will never leave you. Once you give him your problems you have to let it go, and give God the time to work them out. He may not work your problems out when you want him to, but he will work it out for you."

"You're so right. Never again will I doubt him." Jordan grabbed my hand. He looked into my eyes and I could feel the energy that he was giving off. Before I knew it Jordan kissed me. The kiss was so lustful that I surrendered to the urges that I was experiencing.

The kiss that Jordan gave me was electrifying to my senses. I was shocked. That kiss felt really good.

I got out of the car in order to collect myself. Jordan opened the door on the passenger side and asked me to come around. He knew he was getting to me.

I walked to the other side of the car as Jordan asked. He was still sitting down. Jordan pulled me to him and practically laid me down on him. He kissed me so passionately that my body consented to the sensation that he stirred up within me.

Jordan began to rub on me and I became more excited from his touch. This man was doing something to me and I couldn't control it. I tried to resist, but I couldn't, and before I knew it Jordan raised up my dress and glided inside of me.

I couldn't believe what I had just done and what I let happen to me, but I enjoyed every minute of it. I never in a million years ever dreamed of making love in a car, but it was so exciting.

Jordan held me not wanting to let me go. He enjoyed the

time he was spending with me, and he wanted to savor the moment.

I continued to see Jordan whenever he could get away. There were times when I would sneak away to have lunch with Jordan or just to spend some time with him. We had several more times where we had intimate experiences together.

One in particular was when I went up to his job to take him lunch. I went to his office and Jordan was sitting in a chair behind his desk. He asked me for a kiss and I sat on his lap. Jordan was smooth with his hands and again before I knew it I was making love to him in the chair. Again I had a dress on which made it easy for him to enter me. I was afraid that someone would catch us in his office. Hurrying up, I quickly got into my groove and sprayed Jordan as I released my sap.

I was satisfied from another sensual love making experience. Jordan was exposing me to experiences that I had never known or done before. I was enjoying the ride. It had been eight months now that we were seeing each other. I was enjoying every minute of our encounters. I was grateful for every moment I had with Jordan. We had been talking daily on the phone, and he would call me the minute he arrived at work. I would also call in between his counseling sessions, and he would also call before he went home just to say good night if he knew he would not be able to talk to me anymore that night. Jordan would call me every time he had a moment to spare. He was sad when he couldn't talk to me or see me in the evening.

Jordan expressed that he was really getting into me. He said so much that it hurt when he couldn't be with me. Jordan said I was constantly on his mind, and when he gets home he would go to bed right away just to think about me. He wanted to hurry up to go to bed so that the night would be over. He knew in the morning he would be able to talk to me right away and throughout the day. Jordan was visualizing the fantasy world in his mind with me that he knew could never be. He wondered if I felt what he was feeling. I never spoke on how I actually felt about him, and I knew that he would never push the issue. I can tell he wanted me to tell him willingly if I actually felt anything. I was into him as well, but Jordan needed to hear the words that would definitely be embedded in his heart if I felt what he did. He didn't think I was experiencing or feeling what he is going through.

Jordan told me, "There were days when he couldn't eat, or sleep from not being with me. There were days when his heart literally hurt from just not hearing my voice. There were days when he couldn't concentrate on anything but thinking about me. There were days when he needed to make love to me and we couldn't connect. There were days and days of just thinking and wishing that I would never walk out of his life."

Jordan showed that he was jealous that I had another man in my life, but there was nothing he could do about it. He as well was with someone.

He told me there were several times he thought about breaking it off. He was beginning to feel guilty due to the fact that I had nothing but good things to say about Kyder. So, he felt if Kyder is as good a person as I stated, then he shouldn't be falling in love with his woman. He didn't deserve what he was doing to his woman. Jordan realized that this may mean giving me up and walking away. Jordan was a person that was always concerned about someone else being happy. His happiness always came last. So, he thought why should he interfere with our happiness. It really began to bother him, but he couldn't let go. He was in love with me. Jordan realized that all it would take was for me to tell him that I didn't want to give him up, and I wanted to be with him as well. If I was willing to say those words that would be all the confirmation that he would need to hang in there. On the other hand, if I told him that I wanted to be committed to Kyder, he would back away and respect my wishes.

Jordan wondered if he tried to leave would I stop him. I'm sure he would be hurt if I didn't, and he would feel that what we had didn't matter to me one way or another. If I didn't stop him he would surely walk out of my life. All Jordan needed was confirmation by saying the words, "I need you to stay in my life," and I would have a friend in him for as long as I was willing to be involved in this kind of affair.

I could see him looking at me and thinking. He was trying to figure it all out. Jordan felt I made him happy with the little things that I did like our constant telephone talks, and our secret lustful moments. He didn't know if it was due to him not being happy at home or what. He mentioned that he constantly thinks about our connection. Jordan knew that if his relationship did not work out at home and he was to leave today, he wouldn't have a chance with me. Jordan had to face the fact. I would never totally be his.

I never let in on what I was feeling for Jordan. So he wondered if he was merely a toy for me and nothing more.

He could tell that I was really in love with Kyder, by how I spoke about him, and many days it bothered him just to hear anything about Kyder. But he would listen without saying a word wishing that he was the one in his shoes.

Jordan mentioned on several occasions how he and Candice got into arguments and disagreements at home. He wanted so much to leave home, but he knew that it would kill her. Jordan said that Candice would not be able to afford their home on her own. He couldn't see himself leaving her out there struggling. He didn't hate Candice. He just didn't love her anymore and he wanted to be done with the marriage. There was nothing there, and it was getting harder every day faking his feelings.

Jordan claimed he hadn't participated in the relationship for a long time. He said there was no effort on either of their part and now it was really getting to him. Every little thing that she did really irritated him. He knew that Candice was starting to see it as well. He said the other day he was sitting at the table going over some paper work when he dozed off to sleep. Candice came in the kitchen and asked, "Are you going to sleep at the table?" Then under her breath she said 'You really don't want to be anywhere around me." Jordan heard it and asked, "What did you say?" Candice said, "Nothing." So, from her comment he knows that Candice is starting to see how he really feels. Jordan feels that he has become a crutch for Candice. He wants her to start standing on her own. He has done everything for her in the past, and it has really hindered her. Jordan told me there were many things that he had to teach her because she was never exposed to them in her life. For instance, she had no idea on how to write checks or even use the ATM machine. These are just some of the small things that she never learned. Now, because of Jordan, she is learning how to do these things and more.

Jordan keeps pondering on the fact that he doesn't know how long he is going to hang in there. He knows for sure that it's going to end. He just doesn't know when. Then he is wondering where is he going to go? He thought about moving out of the state. Jordan knows that I will probably marry Kyder and he has no plans of ever interfering with our relationship. Jordan would never bring any problems to us. Not now or in the future. He would walk away with a broken heart, but he would let go. So he thought about leaving and moving to another state. It would kill him if he couldn't be with me, but he may have no other choice.

Jordan would have to leave his business and start over. He had some plans in mind for some other things that he wanted to do and he thought maybe he would begin to put those things in motion. That would take his mind off everything for the time being if he is really busy.

Jordan also felt that I may break off everything before Kyder and I get married. He knows that I have my child back, and I will be filing for a divorce from Roscoe. Jordan felt that I would surely marry Kyder right away. He made a statement several times about someone he knows that is messing around. He said, "I have a friend that is having an affair, but sometimes they cool it off then get back together." He wanted to see how I would respond to that statement to see if I would be willing to do the same. If I was thinking about letting go would I come back later?

I remembered one day when we met at a bar and shared hot wings, lamb meat and spicy potatoes. We also had drinks together and were making toasts. Jordan's toast was to "Forever." He wondered if I would really hang in there forever or was it the drinks. I was touched, but wondered if his toast was sincere.

His feelings were all tangled and emotions up in the air. He was *caught up* as well as I. I understood what he was feeling. Neither Jordan nor I had any idea how things were going to turn out. Jordan felt that he would be on the losing end of the stick, and he was in a no win situation. Some days I could tell he was preparing himself for dealing with that when the time came. Jordan knew that it was not going to be easy for him. He was in love with someone he could never have.

Chapter 21

Tayla

I called Kyder on the phone to tell him about my good news.

"Hey you," I said. You're not going to believe this."

"What? Believe what?"

"I have my daughter back."

"That's wonderful Tayla. How did that happen?"

"Zena brought her to me."

"Zena?"

"Yes."

"Thank God. I'm so happy for you."

"I couldn't believe it when Zena called and said she had Kayla. I thought she was playing some kind of sick joke."

Kyder was happy that my daughter was returned to me. He

was also hoping that I could move on with my life now. Even thou he knew I had one more obstacle to cross. That was getting a divorce from Roscoe. Kyder was going to ask me to marry him once my divorce was final. He told me he loved me and he recognized that a while back.

We were hooking up today. Kyder felt he was overdue for spending some time with me. I was so busy lately that he wondered what was going on.

"Hello Mrs. Anderson," he said. "I guess you have put me on the back burner. I haven't seen you in a while. Is this how we're doing things now?"

"No Boo, I'm sorry. I have been so busy lately since Kayla has returned home."

"I understand. Your child comes first. Handle your business and when you find the time I'm sure we'll get together."

"Look Kyder, I have some time now. Would you like me to come by for a while? I'm sure Zena wouldn't mind watching Kayla for me."

"I have a couple of hours before it's time for me to go to the hospital. That would be great."

I did missed spending time with Kyder. I was so busy with Kayla, dancing, and seeing Jordan that my time was starting to run thin. I didn't want that to happen because Kyder was my rock and I really cared about him. I know he is starting to feel some distance from me. So, I know what I have to do. I have to make him feel that I'm still connected with him.

I got off the phone with Kyder and went to Zena's room. I asked Zena if she wouldn't mind watching Kayla for a few. "I want to run by Kyder house and I will be back shortly. Kayla is still taking a nap."

"No problem Tayla. Take your time. I wasn't going anywhere."

"Thanks girl."

I drove over to Kyder's home, which was twenty minutes away from where we lived. I ranged the bell and Kyder answered the door right away.

Kyder was so happy to see me. He grabbed me and immediately planted a big smothering kiss on my lips. Kyder picked me up and carried me into his bedroom as he closed the door with his foot.

This drove me wild. I loved it when he picked me up. It really turned me on. Kyder placed me down on top of his dresser. It was just the right height in order for him to reach me like he wanted to. He began taking my clothing off as he kissed me very deeply. I moaned from the stimulation as I waited in anticipation for what I hoped would come.

Kyder finally got all of my clothing off. He looked into my eyes as he penetrated me with long heavy stokes. I released a groan as the feeling of him entering me stayed in my mind. Kyder picked me up again after several minutes on the dresser. He gently laid me down on the bed and avidly made love to me.

I sensed that Kyder felt that I was somehow losing the bond that we had, and he wanted to keep the fire going. He was unsure why or if it was still due to everything that has been going on in my life. I could tell he was trying to do something quickly to keep me connected. He felt that the more he stays in contact with me the more I'm into him. Whenever we are apart or if he doesn't talk to me, I seem to lose the connection. He has always stated that he never wants to lose me and he planned on doing whatever he had to do to keep me.

CHAPTER 22

Jordan

Merry Christmas and happy holidays were the words spoken in the air today. It was Christmas Eve and I didn't feel happy or merry. It had been a few days since I last saw Tayla, and each time I talked to her it was only for a few minutes before she would state, "Let me call you back." Those words stunned my mind as I anticipated them coming after a few minutes each time. Lately we could never finish a complete conversation before she had to hurry off the phone.

I'm disturbed, confused, and have sullen thoughts from facing the realization of wondering if I could stay involved with her. It's becoming harder by the minute. Some days I feel like I want her to be the one to break things off. I have so many mixed emotions. I don't want to appear as the one who is ending the relationship, but in actuality she is ending it all along with the less and less contact we are having. She seems to be so busy and she doesn't have much time for me.

I was finding it hard not being with her and only talking to her for a few minutes at a time. I know I'm at the end of the list in her life and I'm not sure if I wanted to remain in that position. I never put her at the end of my list. In fact, Tayla is at the top of my list. She has become my everything. The Love we have stays on my mind. My every move is with the thought of how I can incorporate her into my day or week.

I confessed that I loved her but I know she doesn't feel the same love that I feel for her. Yes, she loves me, but I love her more.

I have one friend that knows about our affair. I called my friend Fred for some encouragement. Fred is also having an affair. So, we are able to relate to each other's situation.

"Hey man," I said as Fred answered the phone.

"What's up man?"

"Man, I don't know if I can do this."

"I know man. It get's hard, but you can do it. You come too far to turn back now. I'm hurting too. I didn't get a chance to see my girl either."

I had silent tears, as I tried to talk to Fred. There was no way I was going to let the tears drop while I talked to my Dawg. I had to put on that strong tone to my friend when in fact I was very weak at this moment.

Fred knew what I'm feeling. "Damn man. You love her. You have fallen in love with Tayla. What are you going to do?"

"I don't know. I do know we'll never be together as a couple, and I have accepted that. She is going to marry her guy.

In fact I need her to marry him because if something happens and they don't get married I know I would definitely leave Candice right away. I'm not in love with Candice any more. I know that for sure. I'm just going through the motions. I don't want to hurt Candice, but I'm tired of being unhappy. I plan on ending the marriage, but I want to do it in a good way. I don't know if anyway is a good way, but I want her to be able to take care of herself. I won't leave her in a bad position. I can't do that. I'm making plans to make a move where we both will be stable after I leave."

"Are you sure that you and Tayla will not get together after you leave?"

"Well, I know she will be marrying her guy. I can't see her going through all of that then leaving him. I know she loves him as well. I think I was just an extra outlet for her when she was going through a rough time, but for me it developed into something more. I know that not being with her hurt like hell."

"Man what you need to do is find yourself another woman to help you forget about this woman."

"Naw man, I can't roll like that. I need to get my heart and soul back. I'm too connected to this woman. I see she doesn't have much time for me so that will help me lose some of the connection."

"Do you know for sure that she is trying to lose that connection?"

"She hasn't said it, but action speaks louder than words. I think I have seen her once or twice this month."

"Maybe she is just busy and she can't get to you like she use to."

"I remember her telling me that you make time for what you want to do. Lately, every time I try to hook up it never works out."

"Maybe you guys timing is not right."

"That's possible, but for some reason I feel it's a little more. I also feel that she's keeping me around for something. She doesn't want to totally let me go. I need more. I'm not asking her to leave her guy. I just need a little more time then what she's giving me right now, and lately she tries to make it seem like it's my fault we can't get together. You know the reverse act."

"You need to think about seeing someone else. You know there's plenty more woman out there."

"I know man, but I'm not ready to be with anyone else. If I can't be with her then I think I'm going to cool out and work on putting things in place to end my marriage."

"Man, do you know what you are saying?"

"Yes, I know. I'll be giving up the booty."

"Are you sure you want to do that?"

"I did it a long time ago before I got married. I

can do it again."

"Good luck! You need to really think about this."

"I'll give it some thought and see how things are going before I make a final decision."

"Alright man. If you feel like making a move lets hit the club tonight. You know there were some fine women checking you out at that club on Saturday."

"Yes there were a lot of fine woman, but I want my Boo. I think I'm going to chill tonight."

"If you change your mind let me know."

"Will do. Talk to you later."

I was hurting something awful today. I was in agony and the pain in my heart wouldn't let up.

I was feeling trapped. Trapped in several boxes and trying to figure my way out. I knew if I did what I wanted to do, which was to get out of my marriage, I would feel much better and have a piece of mind. But I kept thinking about everyone else involved. I am a patient person, and I know I would have to wait it out for the sake of everyone.

After I got off the phone with Fred I sat on the couch looking out the window into the snowy night on Christmas Eve, while Candice was running around doing her last minute Christmas chores. The only light on was from the soft glow of the Christmas tree. Normally, the atmosphere of watching the Christmas tree would make me feel festive and romantic, but not today. I had too many emotions going on right now.

I sat there thinking about how I was going to pull myself out of this depression I was falling into.

I was glad that the holidays would be over soon. I needed some alone time from everyone to think. My mind took me directly to thinking about her. I remembered a time when I was complaining to Tayla about not spending enough time together.

She asked me was I getting spoiled.

I responded no. I'm not spoiled, I was addicted. I accept that maybe I was getting use to the constant phone talks and the time we were spending together. Those times always made me happy. She stimulated me mentally and physically. That was one thing I loved about her. I was bored at home, and I craved for the constant talks I was getting from Tayla. It was for a few minutes each time, but I longed for them. She always gave me something to look forward to throughout my day.

Now, she was taking those moments away. I couldn't understand how she could announce to me that she loved me then start changing the routine. My thoughts were that you don't tell a person one day that you love them then change the next day. Unless you're just telling them what you think they want to hear. I didn't want her love this way, and hoped that was not her intentions.

I wondered if this was a game that she was playing with me. I hoped that she was not playing with my emotions.

At this point I figured out what I had to do to protect my heart.

I made up my mind that I would give her what I thought she wanted. I was going to stop calling so much and try not to worry about seeing her. I felt less contact and time apart would initially hurt, but eventually I would be able to deal with the distance. Then it wouldn't hurt as much. I know it's going to be hard and hurt like hell. I felt like not only does she have my heart, but she has my soul as well.

I don't think she realizes the magnitude of my love for her. I think she feels because I'm married and haven't left my wife that I don't really love her. She knows it's not that easy to just walk away. My heart keep telling me to give it all up and walk away, but there are too many factors involved with doing it that way.

I was feeling emotionally and physically neglected, and I thought about telling her we need to talk. I decided against the talk and wanted to wait it out. I didn't want Tayla to see me as being weak, although I was suffocating from not receiving my love.

I decided I would start right away and move back. I was putting my love for her in a box and sealing it up. I felt if it was meant to be, she would unwrap the box and take back my heart.

She knows the love I feel for her would not let me walk away. In the mean time I was going to give her the space that I think she needs and stop whining about not being able to see or spend any time with her. I didn't want to be smothering. I wanted to take advantage of the time we were able to be with each other even though that time was not ample enough for me. It was all that I have and I was not going to mess that up.

I was determined to concentrate on myself for the New Year. I was going to get my body in shape, focus on getting the funds in for my business, take a serious look at my marriage, and put something in place so that I could be happy whether Tayla is with me or not. I'm going to let God guide my life.

I'm tired of not being happy and for the New Year I have plans on working on my own happiness.

CHAPTER 23

Tayla

On Christmas Kyder gave me a ring. The ring was a promise that he would always love me and forever be in my life, and when the time is right he wanted me to be his wife.

I was lost for words. My mind took me back to reminisce on the day we first hooked up. It was crystal clear in my mind. It was a Saturday, on June 21. I remembered Kyder stopping by earlier that day. He had to pick up some information. He would always call me by my last name, Mrs. Anderson. I asked him why he won't call me by my first name since he knows me now. He said. "If I call you by your first name I will have to take you from your husband." I just smiled. He left and later that evening he called me and asked if I would meet him.

I finally agreed. We met in the parking lot of a grocery store about ten that night.

I was surprised that I agreed to meet Kyder. It was out of my character to be meeting any man and especially at that time of night. Normally, I would be at home in my pajamas getting ready for bed, if not already in bed. Tonight I was in the mood for some excitement. I was home alone and it was nice outside. I was feeling adventurous tonight.

Kyder arrived at the parking lot first. I made it and stopped in the middle of the first aisle of the parking lot. I wasn't sure what kind of car Kyder was riding in. I forgot to ask him.

I dialed his number to see if he had arrived. When he answered he said, "Is that what you do stop, in the middle of the aisles?"

I laughed to myself before responding. "No, I was trying to see if you were here before parking."

"I'm in the next aisle."

I drove to the next aisle and parked my car.

Kyder got out of his car and jumped into the passenger seat of my car.

"Hello," he said.

"Hi."

Kyder was at a party and rushed out to meet me for a while. We sat in the car and listen to music and talked. The conversation was nice and the mood was cozy. Just the mere closeness to him was making me hot. I never experienced these feelings before so soon with any man. I wanted to kiss Kyder, but I was afraid of taking that step. He must have felt the connection because he grabbed my hand and held it. Kyder's hand glided over my breast. I suspected that he wanted to see how I would respond. He didn't realize what he was doing to me. I knew at that moment I had to have more of him.

Things were moving very fast. Kyder was unsure if he should have been with me. He knew I was still married and it was out of his character to get involved with a married woman. He asked himself, "What am I doing here?" But he didn't leave. He continued to stay and that was enough for me to know that he wanted to be with me as well. After talking for a while and listening to music, Kyder had to leave. He asked me for a hug. Kyder got out of the car and walked around to my side of the car. I got out and gave him a big hug. I didn't want to let him go. I felt so comfortable while wrapped inside of his strong arms. All I could think of was thank God we're outside in a parking lot. If we had been inside any closed place, only God knows what would have happened that night. I didn't want to end the night. I was enjoying his company and the time I was spending with him. I wanted to stay wrapped in his arms. His touch was spell-binding and I wanted more. From that day we began talking on the phone daily and often several times throughout the day. I came out of my pensive reflection of thinking about how we met. I began to admire the ring that Kyder had given me. I wondered if I gave in and totally gave my love to Kyder would it last. Did he truly love me, I wondered? I was afraid. I was afraid of being hurt again. I had given all of my love to Roscoe and he abused it. I was scared of loving again, and besides, I knew I would have to take care of ending my marriage to Roscoe before I could actually give my love completely.

Kyder was sitting next to the Christmas tree playing with Kayla. It was nice seeing how he became so involved with Kayla, and it warmed my heart to see them interacting together.

He had brought some things for Kayla. Kyder thought I wouldn't have money to give Kayla a nice Christmas, so he wanted to make it special for Kayla and me.

I was sitting back as my mind began to reflect on the reasons I loved him. In my mind I could come up with thirty reasons. I thought about the ones that meant the most to me. I loved Kyder because he could soothe me whenever I was upset. I loved the sound of his voice that was relaxing to my mind. I thought about how Kyder cared about my feelings and about making me happy. I loved it when Kyder would call me first thing in the morning to say Good Morning and at night to say Good Night. I loved looking into his eyes and feeling his heart. I loved the way he handled me when we are talking on the phone or are together. I loved the smell of his body that stayed in my mind whenever he wasn't around me. I loved the way he called my name. I loved meeting him for hugs whenever we couldn't spend quality time together or just when one of us was down. I loved everything about this man, and the only thing that I could think of that I didn't love was that we didn't have enough time to spend together. I needed time with him to feel connected and to feel that he truly loved me. I wasn't seeing him as often as I liked and it was taking a toll on me as well. I was trying not to complain. I began to hold it in because we both had things that were keeping us apart. I would just concentrate on enjoying the time whenever we could get together. This is the least I could do because I wasn't free.

"Hey you. What's on your mind? You seem to be in deep thought over there," said Kyder.

"Oh, I was just thinking about my life. Where I came from and what's been happening so far."

"Are you happy now?"

"Yes, I can say that I'm happy now. I haven't been for a long time. There are some days when I'm down, but for the most part I have been truly happy since I've been with you."

Kyder stood up from playing with Kayla. He walked over to me and grabbed me up in his arms.

He looked deep into my eyes. "Look babe. All I want is for you to be happy. If you're happy then everything else will fall into place. I want to be the man that makes all your dreams come true. I want you to know that I got your back in whatever you need and want. I got you, in whatever your desires are. Please don't hesitate on coming to me for whatever you need. No matter how small or big. Is that understood?"

"Yes Kyder."

Kyder kissed me seductively and whispered in my ear, "I'm yours forever if you would have me."

Those words sent a chill down my spine, and I hoped he meant them.

CHAPTER 24

Jordan

I met up with Tayla today. I was very excited to be spending some time with her. She came by my job before the staff arrived at work. Tayla already knew that she was in for something special due to me being so unpredictable, and she was right. We made love on top of the sink in the bathroom. Everything was going so good and I was happy until I heard the news that I never wanted to hear.

Tayla announced that she would be marrying Kyder next year once her divorce is final. The look on my face showed like someone had stabbed me in my heart. I felt it was coming but actually hearing it was torture. I felt like someone close to me had died. I tried not to let it show because I carry my emotions on my shoulder.

Tayla informed me that Kyder was helping her file for divorce. She said they had one hearing where Roscoe didn't show up. So the judge informed her to put an ad in the newspaper to attempt to find him and inform him about the divorce. If he doesn't show up after the ad the judge will grant her divorce. I think he was given thirty or sixty days to respond.

She said, "As soon as my divorce is final, I will begin planning my wedding. Tayla also told me that getting married wouldn't change our affair. All it would mean is that we both are married.

I was happy to hear what we have wouldn't change, but I was also scared. I was scared that she would change her mind and decide that she was ready to be faithful. She knew if she confessed that to me, the only thing I would be able to do is respect her wishes. In my mind and heart I knew I could never let go, but if she wanted to end it there was nothing I could do to stop her. I recognized that day would eventually come. This only gave me another reason to try and protect my heart.

Tayla appeared excited to be getting married. She said her marriage to Roscoe was a joke. She told me now she would be able to really plan her wedding. She went on and on about the wedding.

I listened, but I could really care less about her getting married. I wished that it was me marrying her. I wished that I could end my marriage to Candice and be with Tayla, but I knew even if I did end my marriage I still would not be able to be with her. It would not be the same. I would not be able to see her when I wanted to and I would still have to go through many heartbroken lonely holidays. I would never have her until dawn or morning light. She would always have to leave to go back to her husband. Those words made my stomach turn. It felt like someone was squeezing and turning my intestines in knots. I was sick. I felt like I wanted to throw up.

I knew that day was coming, but the timing of hearing it was so wrong. I wondered how could I just make love to her then she announced that she was getting married. She must know how I feel about her and why didn't she take my feelings into consideration?

I was at a loss for words. I was hurting from hearing her good news. She had to go and I was glad that she had to leave. I didn't want her to see the pain that I was feeling. Once I left out the door I called my friend Fred.

Fred could tell by the sound of my voice that something was wrong.

"What's the matter man?"

"Man, she just told me that she and her guy are getting married."

"You're lying."

"I wish I was. We just finished making love and I was so excited about seeing her until she dropped that bomb on me."

"Damn Dawg. She could have waited until later to tell you."

"My thoughts exactly, but then again no matter what time she told me I was going to feel the same way."

"Man, you got to release that hold this lady has on you."

"I know, and it's so strange. It's not like we spend a lot of time together. I'm still trying to figure out how I fell in love with her. It's more like we have a phone relationship. We talk so much on the phone daily and several times throughout the day. How do you fall in love that way?"

"You guys have a connection. You know things happen for a reason and maybe it's meant for you and Tayla to have this affair."

"I don't know, but I do know that I love her and I need her in my life."

"Can I be honest with you Dawg?"

"I'm not sure I want to hear it, but go ahead."

"I told you before what you need to do. You need to get another woman to help release that hold she has on you. If you don't you're going to get hurt."

"Naw man. I'm not into all of that. I don't want to mess around with any other women. That's not me. If I can't handle it any more I'll have to let go."

"You won't. You love her too much. She will hurt you before you let her go, then it's going to be too late."

"That's a chance I'm willing to take. I need her in my life right now."

"Why don't you try to make it work with Candice? That will help ease some of the feelings that you feel for Tayla."

"Well, Candice has been trying to make things a little better at home. We had a long talk. She was doing all of the talking. In fact, she asked me to only listen and to think about what she was saying. She didn't want me to respond.

Candice wanted me to think about her conversation and we would talk over dinner Saturday."

"That's a start."

"Yeah, but...."

"I know. Tayla has your heart now."

"My heart and soul."

"That's not good. Man, I don't want to see you get hurt."

"What about you. You're in the same boat. You love your girl."

"Yes I do, but it's different with us."

"Why is that?"

"We have a past. We dated when we were younger. I always loved her, and now that we're back together we vowed to never leave each other again. It gets hard for us, but we just enjoy the time that we're able to be together. We want more, but at this time we know it can't be more and we're willing to deal with it as long as we're together. Some days we can't get together like we plan and she is ready to quit me. But I know she's not going anywhere. She also knows that I'm not going anywhere. Sometimes I want to leave home to be with her. We both know we can't right now, and we would feel worst if we end it."

"I know I will feel worst if we couldn't be together also. I don't want to ever think about not being with her. You're right. I'm going to try and relax a little. I don't want to stress her out. One person stressed out is enough. I have to accept it as it comes and don't worry about what doesn't happen. I never want or will bring any problems to her."

"Does she make you happy?"

"Yes, being with her and talking to her daily on the phone makes me happy."

"Then go with the flow. You never know what the future holds. Just hold on to what you have right now and enjoy her while you have the chance."

"You're right Dawg. Thanks for the advice."

"I'm just returning the favor. You kept me grounded when I

didn't hear from my girl that time. I was about to lose my mind and you talked me through it. If it wasn't for you I don't know what I would have done."

"So, are you all good?"

"Yeah, I'm good. All I can do is take it one day at a time."

"I agree."

CHAPTER 25

Tayla

I was finally about to be a free woman. Roscoe still hasn't responded to the newspaper article. I had not heard or seen Roscoe in several months. I hoped that Roscoe had given up on us, but I knew I would still have to be careful, knowing Roscoe.

I was closing that chapter in my life with Roscoe. I was getting ready to open up a new book with Kyder. One that I felt was going to be stimulating with an abundance of happiness.

I wasn't forgetting about Jordan. He was making me happy by providing my life with plenty of excitement. I enjoyed the time we spent together, but I knew Jordan had ties that he would not be able to let go. I didn't want to be the one that break up his marriage. I was trying to convince him to not let go, and to stay with his wife. I knew that I could never give up Kyder. Not for him or anyone else. So, if he wanted to be a part of my life then he would have to understand and accept that I was marrying Kyder.

I didn't want to give up Jordan, but if it means losing Kyder I would give him up in a heartbeat. Kyder was my world now and I was excited by the new changes he would be bringing into my life.

Another month passed and I still didn't hear from Roscoe. I didn't waste any time buying bridal magazines right away because I knew I would be getting a divorce soon. Kyder and I were sitting down every chance we got to sketch out wedding plans. We both were so excited.

Kyder was very involved in all the plans. It was surprising to me to see him so involved. I thought normally men would sit back and let the woman do all the planning, but not Kyder. He wanted to show me how serious he was about the wedding. Kyder was giving his opinion and ideas on everything down to the color. I was happy to see that he was taking a big part in the planning process.

There were many times I would speak about my wedding plans to Jordan, and he would listen without saying a word. We have a relationship where we can talk about any and everything, but I think the whole idea of talking about the wedding really bugged him.

He would never be rude about the conversation, but would always find a way to change the subject.

I would tell him how Kyder is so excited about the wedding and getting married, but Jordan felt in his heart that I was the one that appeared excited to him.

Jordan mentioned that he felt there would never be anything with us where I would be that excited. I know he just wanted it all to be over and done with. He never said it but I know he didn't want to hear about the wedding or the wedding plans and it really bothered him. I'm sure he was only concerned about me coming back from the honeymoon. I could tell that he wanted to know if I would still want him in my life after the wedding.

Jordan would never bring up this issue to me. He would wait and see what happens. He told me that he wasn't going to complain or make an issue out of anything that happens with us anymore. He said he is going to let everything play itself out because time will reveal it all.

He felt if our relationship doesn't change when I return from my honeymoon, then he has a chance of remaining in my life. He kept telling me that he would have to find a way to protect his heart until he finds out if he's in it for the long haul.

Jordan was still talking to me daily, but it was still hard seeing each other. He asked me to give him four to five hours one Saturday. We haven't had that much time together in a long time. I said "I got you." Jordan didn't think it was going to happen. He didn't think I was going to be able to pull it off.

On Wednesday Jordan asked me if we were still on for Saturday. I informed him that I would have to let him know because I may have something to do for the wedding on Saturday. I told Jordan, "Remember I said I might have something to do, but I couldn't remember what?"

Jordan said this was starting to happen lately. He said I would say remember I told you I might have something to do when in fact he said I never even mention that to him. He took it as his key to see that it was not going to happen. He just played it off and said okay.

I began to see that he was not going to ask me when we were going to hook up anymore. Again, he was going to wait it out and see what happens. If we hooked up he thought that would be wonderful, and if we didn't he wouldn't be disappointed because he won't be expecting it. Jordan was acting like he was on an emotional roller coaster with me. He mentioned that sometimes I made him feel as though I loved him, then other days he didn't know what to think about my love. Jordan appeared afraid, but he wouldn't let go.

One Friday I called him and the first thing he said was, "Can I have my Friday's back?" On Friday's after Jordan got off from work we would hook up and have drinks and talk. Jordan enjoyed the Fridays as well but they weren't happening anymore.

I know he was wondering if things would go back to how it use to be after the wedding, or is this the sign to let him know he needs to get out before he really gets hurt.

Jordan seemed so excited to be hooking back up on Fridays.

You could hear in his voice that he was happy knowing he would be spending an hour or two with his Boo. I'm sure that was constantly on his mind.

Jordan was in high spirits today because he was meeting up with me at my house.

He called and asked me how much time I had. He wanted to go to the hotel instead of my place. He didn't want Zena to walk in. Jordan said he wanted to be relaxed while making love to me. He suggested that we get a room.

I told him to come over to my place. Jordan said he would call to see if it's clear to come once he got off of work.

At six o'clock Jordan got off and called as he said he would.

I told him again to come on over.

When he arrived things instantly began to heat up. Jordan took off his coat and went to work. He was a man that knew what he wanted. He kissed me then pulled down the jogging pants I had on. Jordan lifted me up and placed me on the kitchen sink. He slowly entered me as I began to moan from the excitement. I was ready to be fully made love to. I was making so much noise from the excitement that Jordan said, "You act like this is the first time we made love." I was caught up in the thrill of it all and it really turned me on. I thought about how in movies you see people making out on the sink. I got the thought in my mind about turning the water on and letting it drizzle down our body. Then again I didn't want to send him home wet.

He noticed the flickering glow of the candle coming from the bedroom. He was getting ready to lift me off the sink and carry me into the bedroom until I announced that I had to leave shortly. Jordan said he thought he was going to be spending some real quality time with me. He appeared very disappointed. I could tell he wanted the chance "to do what he do." Jordan knew how to pull several orgasms out of me whether we spend one, two, three or four hours together.

I stated I had to meet up with Kyder at a friend's house. He was waiting on me.

Jordan said he wasn't expecting a quickie today, nor did he want one. He stated he needed more because he hadn't been feeling me lately, and he really needed this connection today. Jordan asked me for a towel so he could wash up and leave.

I gave him a towel and he cleaned up without saying a word. Jordan appeared pissed, and he was trying to keep it to himself.

After he washed up he went back into the kitchen and sat in a chair. The look on his face said he couldn't believe our Friday was ending this way.

"Let's have a shot of Tequila," he asked.

"Okay, what are we toasting to?"

He whispered, "Better times."

I loved it when Jordan made the toast. He always knew what to say.

Jordan was sitting in the chair without saying a word.

"What's on your mind?" I asked.

"Nothing! Let me get going since you have something else on your agenda."

Jordan got up to leave. He opened the door and walked out without saying a word or even looking back. Today he didn't hug, kiss me or even say goodbye as he left out the door.

A few minutes later he called me on my cell phone. I could tell he had to get it off his chest.

"You telling me you just found out that you had to meet him?"

"Yes, he just called while you were on your way over."

"There was no way you could have told him that you had to make a stop first then you would meet him?"

"No, Jordan. I couldn't."

"I see."

Jordan was finding it hard to believe that I just found out. He felt I knew all along and I was just trying to squeeze him into time I didn't have to keep him from complaining. I believe Jordan would have felt better or even understood if I told him up front what I had to do then he could have made the decision if he still wanted to come over or not.

"I wished we could have had a little more time together."

"I'm sorry Jordan. There was nothing I could do."

Jordan really didn't want to argue, so he said, "I'll talk to you later."

Jordan felt he was listening well and nothing was said about me meeting Kyder. He stated he listens to every word that comes out of my mouth. In fact, many times he plays back our conversation in his mind. Jordan revealed that he holds on to every piece of contact he receives from me. He told me several times that I occupy so much of his mind space and heart. That's why it hurts a lot of times when he can't be with me.

I called Jordan back on his cell. "Look Jordan, you already knew what to expect when you got into this relationship. I'm not going to be stressed out this year, and besides I have too much to lose."

The quietness on the phone told me that those words hit Jordan hard like a hammer.

"Damn" Jordan said. "Too much to lose. I never wanted to or tried to jeopardize Kyder and your relationship, and I'm sure you know that is something I would never do. So, how could you even throw that in my face? And what about me? Do you feel that I'm too much to lose?"

"Of course Jordan. You know how I feel about you."

"I'm not sure that I do."

Jordan said he was hurt that the evening ended this way. He revealed that his heart literally began to hurt.

Jordan was quiet for a moment.

"Hey what's up?" I asked.

"I'm just trying to compose myself. My heart hurts so bad that

I hope I'm not having a heart attack. I have never felt this way about anyone in my life, not even my wife."

"Jordan you got to get yourself together or surely you are going to have a heart attack."

Jordan said "let me let you go. I have another call. Besides, I need a couple of minutes to collect myself."

Jordan hung up the phone.

I missed a call from Tayla. My phone beeped again and I thought it was Tayla calling me back. It was Fred on the line.

"Hey man, what's up?"

"Man, I just left Tayla and it wasn't good."

"Oh you guys had a fight," joking Fred.

"And it wasn't nice. Man my heart is hurting so bad."

"Man, those women are going to give us a heart attack."

"I know. So, what's up with you?"

"I was calling to see if you were home. I was going to stop by."

Fred lived two doors down from me.

"I'll be there in ten minutes."

"Good. I'll see you then."

I made it home and there was no one there. Candice and Justice went over to her mother's house.

As I was hanging up my coat my phone rang. It was Fred telling me to open up the door. We always left the door unlocked when we knew one of us was coming over.

Fred came in and went straight to the living room. He sat on the couch and turned the television on to a sports channel. I walked into the living room and asked Fred if he wanted a drink.

"Yeah man. That would be nice."

I grabbed two shot glasses, the tequila and went into the living room.

We sat and talked about the women in our lives.

Fred was saying how he really needed to see his girl, and he hadn't talked to her today. He was stressing and said how pissed he was she hadn't called him.

I said, "I'm mad, about the whole ordeal today. I think I'm through."

"Man, stop fooling yourself. You know you're not through with her," Said Fred.

"I am. I'm so through."

"You're not through. You're just pissed."

"I'm trying not to worry about things that I know I can't control. If I can't change what's making me sad, then it's time to move on."

"You know Tayla is not going to let you quit her Man," said Fred.

"I don't know. She told me she was not going to be stressed out and she got too much to lose."

"Wow, that's deep."

"I never wanted to stress her out or make any problems for

them. So, I was really surprised to hear her say that to me. You can't imagine how that made me feel. So maybe I just need to leave her alone."

"You know you don't want to give her up."

"I don't. I need her in my life."

"Everything will work out. Don't make any hasty moves that you know you will regret later."

"Yeah, you're right Dawg. I just need to calm down. If she would have just called back and said, "I'm sorry things didn't work out as you hoped, and I love you. It would have made me feel better. She knows how to soothe me."

"She wasn't thinking about soothing you because she got upset herself."

"So forget it Dawg. Neither you nor her is going anywhere."

"We'll see. I'll let things cool down and give her a call tomorrow."

"That may be best."

Fred finally received a call from his girl while he was at my house. He was so excited. He talked to his girl and she told him she was sick and her husband was home all day. So she couldn't call.

Fred told her he was going to get her when he sees her for making him worry. They talked for an hour before they got off the phone. Fred went home an hour after his call.

I decided I was going to bed. I wanted the night to hurry up and be over so that I could call Tayla in the morning and work everything out.

I hoped that she would forgive me for my behavior. After thinking about it, I felt I was being a little selfish. I was only thinking about my wants and needs when in fact I know that Kyder comes first.

I never had an affair before. I'm just beginning to learn the rules of the game. My understanding is that my wants, needs, feelings and anything else related to me will come last with Tayla. I believe that's the way it is and the way it will be if I want to be with her. I'm trying so hard to keep my emotions intact.

Chapter 26

Jordan

I took some time to engage my thoughts about the relationship I had with Tayla. The best way I could see it was like a game, and I wasn't winning. I was content to remain in the game, but I felt I was in a losing position. Lately, everything has been going wrong. There were only quick contacts and brisk love making experiences, and I didn't want to focus on the inner emptiness I was experiencing.

I had initially indicated that I wanted my Friday's back, but they still weren't happening. We had plans to hook up on Friday, and I felt it wasn't going to happen. I felt it in my heart. I even turned down going out with my boys so that I could spend some time with Tayla. I wanted to ensure and focus upon building up some real quality time with her, but things didn't work out that way.

On Friday, I got dressed for work. I put on my black pants and a black sweater. I wanted to look good for Tayla. I even got a lot of complements at work on how nice I looked. I had plans on doing something real special and exotic. I didn't want this

Friday to be an unremarkable night. I sense that it was time to move up a level in the game to keep the fire going, and I wanted to reveal some of my sexual cravings.

I called Tayla on her cell phone around the time she got off from work, and she was unable to be reached. I thought maybe she was in meetings all day and unable to return my call. I waited and waited and still she didn't call. I acknowledged that it wasn't happening at this point.

So I called my boy and told him I didn't think it was happening tonight with us. Fred told me to come out with them to a strip joint, and then they were going to hit the club. I declined the offer.

I often presented myself as strong, but it was killing me inside that we didn't hook up. I didn't want to annoy Fred with how I was feelings. So I held my feelings inside.

I was hurt that she had failed to consider my feelings regarding hooking up. She could have at least given me a call to cancel. It hurt me that she didn't want to be with me as I thought she did, or she would have made it happen.

I was learning the rules of the game. The first rule is never make someone a priority when all you are to them is an option. The second rule is their mate will always come first. I was able to deal with this rule. It was the thoughtlessness about not calling to cancel that bothered me.

The third rule of the game is to never fall in love. You can't think of the game as a relationship. It will never be one. I fully understood the rules of the game now, and I had to learn fast.

Tayla called me the next day to inform me that she was having problems with her phone. I only listened. I didn't make a comment one way or another, and I wasn't going to express how I felt. I was sticking to not complaining anymore. No matter how much it hurt. I was planning on taking back my heart to remain in the game.

Tayla's conversation with me was very brief before I had to go. So, I couldn't express myself on how I felt. Then again, I was glad. I didn't want to complain. My memory reminded me that she had a lot going on in her life. I could see there was very little room for me. I thought about letting her have her time until after the wedding to see if things would get better for us.

I hoped that I wouldn't often feel this way. I knew I would always be second or last in her life, and that's just how it is when you're the other man.

I had to ask myself if I could handle being in that position. I believed I could as long as I knew and felt that she still loved me. There were times when she would say things that made me want to stay in that position forever. Then there were times when I wanted to let go, but my heart wouldn't let me.

She told me one day, "I'm not going anywhere." Those words meant a lot to me. My heart did a dance as she released the words from her mouth. I really needed to hear that, and I felt in my heart that she meant it.

I wished that every now and then she would convey those words to me. That would be all I need to remain in the game, besides her love, and her making love to me. I felt if she could do those three things she could have me forever.

I decided I would no longer express to her that I loved her. I wanted to shout yes. Yes I loved you so much that my heart hurt that we can't be together. I yearn for her love. My strong feelings for her are the reason why I'm hurting so much. I was trying to make our affair out of a relationship. I know that it could never be more then what it is now. I told her if at times I'm appearing distant or if she's feeling that I'm trying to quit her that's not the case. I'm just learning how to deal with our affair and take it at face value. I will be a little hesitant in giving my full love. This will be the only way I cannot be hurt any more. If we're going to be involved, then I have to step back a little to protect my heart. I'm learning and I feel that I'm just about there with being able to deal with our affair so it doesn't hurt anymore if I don't see Tayla.

Tayla told me something that made a lot of sense, and hopefully it would keep me from worrying so much. She told me, "You can't worry about things you can't change." Those words made me think and see the light. I felt I was going to take that advice. My plan was to deal with our affair on a day to day basis and just enjoy the time that we are able to spend together. I perceived that things will never happen as my heart hoped they would. So, in order for me to stay in the game I have to take the present as it comes. I hoped that the present would be enjoyable for me, and not stressful. I didn't want to experience any negative emotions from our affair. I wanted to identify more with feelings such as happiness and excitement in order for me to want to stay in the game. I knew my emotions were caught up and I couldn't let go.

***

Months had passed and things had been going well with Tayla and me. We were hooking up and seeing each other often. I was so happy. We were having eight to ten constant phone talks throughout the day. She had become a needed part of my life in order for me to make it through the day. I was feeling that it was almost too good to be true. I was really into

Tayla and I was able to maintain home as well.

I wanted to keep our relationship spicy in order to keep her interested. She knew that I was excited about her being spontaneous and my manhood was always ready and at attention as soon as she took her clothes off.

CHAPTER 27

Tayla

I was in the grocery store picking up items for dinner. I was in the rice and pasta aisles when I heard a voice that sounded very familiar to me. I stopped abruptly hoping the person I heard was not who I suspected. I listened again very closely this time. I got nervous and all of a sudden I left my buggy in the aisles attempting to leave the store. I began to run to the front of the store and almost tripped over a box of Zataran's red beans and rice. I stumbled to the front of the aisle and ran dead into a man. He held me to keep me from falling. As I looked up I looked right into the eyes of Roscoe.

Frantically, I tried to pull away from Roscoe grasp.

He continued to tighten his grip on my arm as he smiled up at me. Again I tried to pull away.

"Not so fast," said Roscoe quietly. He held on to my arm and led me out of the store.

Roscoe led me to his car. He attempted to make me get in.

"Get your ass in the car!" He said through clenched teeth. We have some unfinished busy to deal with."

I was reluctant to get in the car. I knew that if I got in Roscoe was going to surely hurt or kill me.

Roscoe tried to push me in the car.

I begin to pull back and resist Roscoe's demands. I made up in my mind that I was not going without a fight. I knew that either way Roscoe was going to give me hell. I thought if he was going to kill me if he had to do it in the grocery store parking lot. I was not going to allow him to take me away to hurt me. I began fighting back and that surprised him.

Roscoe took one hand and hit me across my face.

"Bitch! I know you don't think you can whip me." Roscoe hit me again in my face.

I remembered the last beating I received from Roscoe, so I attempted to protect myself and instantaneously I kneed Roscoe in the balls. He immediately released the grip he had on me. I began to scream for help as I was running through the parking lot. I notice a security car that was monitoring the lot and I flagged him down. He noticed me and came over. I informed him of what had just occurred. Roscoe saw me talking to the security guard and finally managed to get himself together to get in the car. He got away while I was talking to the guard.

A lady walked over and gave us Roscoe license plate number. The lady said, "I saw you struggling with that man as I was taking down his license plate number you got away."

"Thank you," I said. As the lady passed the number to me then left.

I was asked to stay to complete a police report. The guard

and I were going into the office to see if we saw anything on the security camera. The security guard asked me to follow him inside to the office. I was glad to be going back inside. I didn't know if Roscoe was still around somewhere waiting for me to leave. I didn't want him to follow me home.

Once inside the security office, the officer pulled up different areas in the parking lot. I began to show him where the car was parked. I remembered the area because my own car was parked in the same aisle four cars down.

The camera captured Roscoe and me in the lot. The picture was clear as it showed Roscoe leading me to the car and being forceful with me. The guard saw me trying to resist and Roscoe hitting me.

"This is your ticket to freedom," said the guard.

I got nervous as I looked at the re-current events of Roscoe attacking me.

The guard noticed my nervousness. "It's okay lady. You can have him arrested with this tape."

I tried to get myself together. "I need to make a phone call," I announced.

I wanted to call Zena and Kyder to inform them of what happened. I was hoping that one of them would be able to drive my car home for me.

I called Zena who picked up right away.

"Hello Zena," Is all that I could get out before I started crying.

"What's going on Tayla?" asked Zena.

I began to cry again. "I ran into Roscoe at the grocery store and he tried to force me into his car. There was a struggle and I manage to get away."

"Where are you now, Tayla?"

"I'm still at the grocery store. I'm too shaken up to drive. I was going to call Kyder to see if he would pick you up so you can drive my car home."

"No problem, Tayla."

I hung up the phone and dialed Kyder line.

It took him a while to answer the phone. I knew Kyder was sleep due to doing his regular sixteen hours at the hospital. Kyder finally answered his phone after several rings.

"Hello Kyder."

He could tell by the tone of my voice that something was wrong.

"Tayla is everything okay?"

I ran down the events that occurred with Roscoe. I asked Kyder if he would come to the store and bring Zena with him.

I could hear him hurriedly jumping up and getting dressed. He told me he was on his way. I'm sure Kyder called Zena directly after getting off the phone with me.

"Hello Zena. Did Tayla call you?"

"I just got off the phone with Tayla. Can you believe what Roscoe did?"

"I'm not surprised, but I wanted to let you know that I'm on my way to pick you up."

Kyder got angry while talking to Zena. "If that monster hurt Tayla in anyway. I promise it will be me and him."

"Look Kyder. Tayla has enough going on. You need to the let the police handle it from here."

"You're right Zena, but…."

"No Kyder. We don't need you sharing a cell with Roscoe."

"I hear you Zena. Are you ready? I should be there in about ten minutes."

"I'll be waiting. See you when you arrive. Bye."

In exactly ten minutes Kyder was pulling up in front of Zena's home. He didn't have to blow the horn. Zena had the door open and was watching out for him. She came right out and got into the car. Zena had asked her next door neighbor to watch Kayla. She had already dropped her off there.

Kyder took off in a hurry once Zena got into the car. I'm sure he didn't want to waste any more time getting to me.

They arrived at the store and rushed inside.

Zena asked one of the cashiers where the security office was located.

They were directed to the location of the security office and immediately headed that way.

When they arrived I was sitting down talking to the officer, and holding ice against my face that had started to swell.

Zena covered her mouth with her hand after talking one look at me. She didn't want to get Kyder more upset.

It didn't help because he lost it when he saw me. Kyder grabbed me with one hand and began hitting the wall with his other hand.

The security guard informed him that he needed to calm down.

"I suggest you get your emotions intact so that we can handle this in the best interest of Tayla," said the guard.

"I'm okay, Kyder. I probably look worst then I feel. Please calm down baby. I just need Zena to drive my car home. Is that okay with you Zena?"

"Sure, Tayla it's not a problem. Is there anything else you need to do here?" asked Zena.

"No, I think we are done here. A lady got Roscoe's license plate number so now we have an address. I'm going to put a restraining order on him, and charge him for the battery against me, continue with the divorce proceedings and file for full custody of Kayla. We have him on tape attacking me. The tape will be a big help in getting everything I want."

"Well, it's going to work out after all. I'm just glad that you were able to get away from him and he didn't hurt you more then he just did," said Kyder.

"Me too because it could have been worse. I'm okay now. I was shaken up a little bit but I'm good now that you guys are here."

"That's good Tayla. Let's get you home so you can clean up yourself and the good doctor here can look you over," said Zena.

"Thanks for all your help," said Tayla to the guard.

"That's what I'm here for. The tape will be ready for your court date. So you take care of yourself. Your husband will be picked up and arrested shortly. He won't be able to harm you any longer. As long as you press charges he will be going to jail."

"Thanks again for your help," everyone said.

We left the security office and headed to Zena's house.

Shortly after arriving home I decided I wanted to take a bath and clean up before seeing Kayla. As I was taking my bath Kyder made me some tea to relax. He turned it on low to keep it warm until I finished with my bath.

Kyder sat down and waited patiently for me to finish my bath. He was in deep thought by the time I had finished my bath. He was hoping that all this abuse was not going to have a long term effect on me. Kyder was thinking so hard that he didn't notice that I had come out of the bathroom.

"Yo," I said bringing Kyder out of his deep thought.

"Hey, how do you feel?" he asked.

"I'm good Kyder, but I'm sure I will be sore tomorrow."

"Why don't you get dressed and I'll look you over."

"Okay baby. Give me a minute."

I went into the room and put on something comfortable. After a few minutes I came out and Kyder checked me over.

"You're going to be a little discolored for a few days, but nothing is broken," he said.

"I'm glad to hear that and I'm glad this will all be over soon," said Tayla.

"Me too," responded Kyder.

***

Several weeks passed and I finally received a letter about coming to court for Roscoe. The court date was only a week away. It was good news to me. I was nervous the whole week. I guess it was the idea of seeing Roscoe face to face again.

The court date arrived and Kyder and Zena went to court with me. They were my support.

I was stunned when Roscoe got off on some technicality but the restraining order was issued for five years, and the divorce was finalized with full custody of Kayla granted to me.

We watched in amazement as the judge gave the order. I only hoped this was the end of Roscoe.

CHAPTER 28

Tayla

"Good morning, Tayla," Jordan said. As he called me on his way to work this morning. This was our normal routine every morning. It always started my day off right. Each day when I saw his number come up on my cell phone I would have the biggest smile plastered on my face. I longed for his call each and every morning. They have become a much needed part of my day.

Jordan and I would talk several times throughout the day. There were many times when we would meet for lunch. Some of those days would be for lunch, while other days it was because we were feeling each other and needed a quick touch of love.

Jordan knew I was trying to keep up with seeing both of them, and some days it would become so hard for me to do.

Today Jordan called me around ten-thirty.

"Hey, am I going to see you for lunch today?" He asked.

"I think I can arrange that.

"When you leave out give me a call." He said.

"Okay, Jordan."

I finished up an assignment I was working on, so that I could be finished by noon. I knew I would probably reach Jordan by twelve-thirty.

On my way over, I called Jordan to let him know I was leaving out. He told me to call once I pull into the parking. I was so excited that I would be spending a little time with him. Today, I didn't care if we were going to be eating or just spending some quality time together. I was just glad that it was happening.

I wore a dress on purpose. I had suspected that he was going to try and see me today. I knew that wearing a dress drove him wild, and it also made easy access for him to relieve me.

I called Jordan on the phone when I pulled into the lot and parked my car.

"I'll be out in a minute," he said.

When he came out he looked at me and said, "And you wore a dress?"

"Where are we going?" I asked.

"Make a right here and follow the road," he said.

It was a nice summer day, so Jordan took me to a park.

I parked the car and Jordan asked, "You want to sit in the park?"

We got out the car and walked over to the playground area. Jordan leaned up against a wooden plank. I walked up to him and leaned up against his body. We kissed and instantly, I got wet. We looked around and two children were riding their bikes through the playground area. Jordan looked around and spotted an empty bench several feet away from the playground.

"Let's go and sit on the bench," he said.

We walked over to the bench holding hands and he sat down.

"Sit on me," he asked.

I sat on him while facing him. My body straddle him as we sat on the bench. I gave Jordan a long slow kiss as he held me tightly.

"I want to get in that" said Jordan as he whispered in my ear.

I responded in a low tone, "What are you waiting for?"

I had become sexually bold when dealing with this man. I have to admit that he was doing something to me as well. Something that was bringing out another side of me that no one would believe if I told them. All of it was wild and exciting.

Jordan told me, "You should have taken your panties off in the car.

"Don't you know how to move them over?"

My wide skirt was very loose and it was draped over Jordan and me. It was very easy for us to get busy. If anyone came by they would think I was just sitting on him.

Jordan went to work and eased inside of me. He was saying something to me in a low seductive tone. I couldn't remember or understand what the hell he was saying because at this moment he was feeling good inside of me.

I could tell it wasn't comfortable for him because he couldn't pull his pants down. So, his zipper was probably causing him some problems, but he didn't stop rolling until he made sure that I was satisfied. That's something I loved about him. It wasn't all about him. He wanted to make sure that I was happy. If I was happy then he was satisfied.

We quickly finished up and Jordan pulled out a couple of napkins to clean up a little. I had wipes in the car that helped us to finish cleaning ourselves up.

We went back to the car and took off. Jordan said he wanted to stop at the store to get something to drink before heading back to work. I drove to a gas station and he went inside and got us both something to drink.

I dropped Jordan off back at work and headed home.

"Call me on your ride home," said Jordan.

These were the sweetest days. There were many like this where Jordan and I would hook up for a few when we needed just a little of each other. Then there were days when we had more time to devote to each other. All of those moments we spent together were good, and kept us hooked together. Besides, we had established a bond and said no matter what we would always be friends.

I wondered if that was true. Could we always remain friends?

CHAPTER 29

Jordan

Candice and I were going through some deep shit. She was riding me about not being home enough. It was really a tough time for me. We had started sleeping in separate bedrooms. It was like two strangers living in the same household. Anyone could tell how tense it was in the house and I didn't know how much longer I was going to be able to stand it.

One thing that kept me there was that Candice had started having medical problems and I knew I couldn't just leave her at this moment. I wanted to be there for Candice to help her through her rough time.

I didn't want her to be stressed out about me, but I knew I could not give up seeing Tayla either.

Candice was the one who told me that she wanted a divorce. I agreed. I was not going to fight it in fact, I welcomed it. I was just waiting to let her do whatever she was going to do.

Every day it was something with Candice. Every move I made outside the house Candice would get upset.

We weren't having sex any longer and this was another thing that bothered Candice.

I couldn't see myself sleeping with her with all the problems we had. It was sure to make things worse and not better. I didn't have the feelings or the desire to sleep with Candice. I just wanted out.

Every night when I went to bed I would fantasize about Tayla. I would lay in the bed for hours thinking and wishing that we could be together. I saw no way that was going to happen. Not now or ever.

I believed if Tayla was free I would definitely give my life up with Candice right away. Since she was not, I felt there was no reason to rush things.

I was two minutes from telling Candice that I was through and ready to leave the marriage. So I thank God that she spoke on it first. I felt the only thing that was holding me back was that I knew that Kyder and Tayla were getting married, and I wouldn't be in her life like I wanted to be.

So I hung in there with Candice trying to stay cool. I didn't want to put any more stress on her since I knew she had some medical problems.

All the while, the only thing I could think of was Tayla. I didn't care what was going on in my home. In fact, I didn't even care if Candice never talked to me. I just wanted to be free to be able to see Tayla when I could, or should I say whenever she was able to see me. I knew if I was free she could have access to me in my own place.

My place could be her escape and unwind place to just hang out and chill.

She always talked about having some other place to go and chill out at. I want to have that available for her whenever she needs it.

My mind can't think of anything else but Tayla. See how I just forgot I was talking about Candice?

Candice was making plans for me and her to get a divorce. I was letting her do it her way. I felt I could live with myself knowing she was the one that initiated and filed for the divorce. Our marriage was definitely over. We talked it out and it was agreed that I would move out of the house.

The plan was that I would continue to help Candice with some of the bills so that it wouldn't be so hard on her. We had settled it all peacefully.

I was happy that everything seemed to be going well. Now, I have to find an apartment. I was excited about being on my own and for the fact that I would be open to see Tayla whenever I was free.

I sat on the couch after my talk with Candice. I wondered could this be real. It was unbelievable that it was finally happening. I speculated on being free and living alone in my apartment. I was glad that I would finally have peace of mind. I also mused over the idea that I would be able to spend more time with Tayla. I began to launch into this fantasy world of us in the midst of splendor and lustful moments. My mind stepped out of the box and opened up to a whole new world.

I reflected on the idea of how I wanted to make love to Tayla. In my mind I invited her over. Once she arrived and stepped through the door, I pinned her up against the wall. We kissed and grinded on the wall until I began to undress her. I lifted her up as I was stepping out of my pajama pants. I was ready as always, and without delay I went to work. I carried her into my exercise room and delicately sat her down on my work bench.

I took my hand and put it into the small of Tayla's back. I bent her over like she was doing a back flip as her whole body was face up. Her hands were flat on the floor while her butt was still on the work bench and her feet were flat on the floor as well. The work bench was kind of low and I was tall. So I had to bend down on my knees as I edged up to Tayla. On my knees I was just the right height as I raised Tayla legs and entered her. "What a work out," was all I could think of.

I snapped out of my reflection at that moment. I was sweating from the mere thought of the scene that was in my mind. "Boy, that seemed so real," I said. "I got to get it together. I haven't even left home yet and here I am thinking about being with Tayla."

I knew I needed to be concentrating on putting things in place at home, but I couldn't keep my mind off of her. I got up once so I could clear my mind of any notion about Tayla. I knew I had business to take care of and thinking about her was not helping me.

Candice walked into the house as soon as I got up off the couch. She noticed a strange look on my face.

"What is it?" she asked.

"What do you mean? What is it? I said.

"You look like you wanted to say something."

"No, I think we have said it all, but I do need to tell you that I will be looking for an apartment."

"Do what you have to do, Jordan," snapped Candice.

"I thought this was what you wanted," asked Jordan.

"No, this is what you wanted Jordan. Let's not play games. It's obvious that this marriage is over and has been for a while. Let's not continue the charade any longer."

"I agree. That's why I'm making plans to move out. I think we both have been through enough and we should be moving on with our lives."

"It's a shame that we had to get to this point, but it is what it is," said Candice.

"Yes it is."

"And what are your plans as far as the church?"

"I will be leaving and finding another church. I think that would be best for the both of us."

"I see."

"I don't want you to be uncomfortable and we don't need the talk."

"You mean you don't need the talk because it won't be me they are talking about but you."

"Whatever the case may be Candice. We don't need the drama nor do I want it."

"Well tell me Jordan. Is it another woman?"

I didn't want to lie, but I knew I would never admit to it being another woman in my life. I didn't want to hurt Candice and I wouldn't let any problems come to her.

I held my head up as I began to tell this lie. "No, Candice, our problems have nothing to do with another woman. I think we fell out of love with each other a long time ago. I guess neither one of us wanted to be the first to say goodbye."

"So why now?"

"Like you said, we played charades long enough. I think we both will be happy and less stressed once everything is final."

Candice didn't make a comment back. She looked at me then turned and walked away. A few minutes later she came back into the room.

"How soon will you be leaving?"

"As soon as I find a place."

Candice grabbed her purse and slammed the door as she walked out.

CHAPTER 30

Tayla

Jordan and I hooked up Saturday night. We went to a birthday party that one of his friends had. Jordan was already at the party when I arrived. He was surprised that I came. It was hard for us to spend a Saturday night together because of our partners.

We ended up having a nice night together. Jordan felt very special because I decided to do something with him and I gave up my Saturday night with Kyder. Lately there was something going on either every Friday or Saturday with Kyder and I. So, Jordan was on top of the world and he was really feeling me tonight. We played a game of spades against another couple and won two games. Jordan and I were drinking 1800 tequila that he brought to the party so we were feeling good. That was our choice drink together.

After the card game we went outside to get some air and to be alone for a while. It was a little cool outside, but to us the night was beautiful as we stood outside and talked from our hearts as the stars twinkled above our heads.

Jordan was bursting with love for me, and it showed by the way he looked deeply into my eyes and tenderly held my hand. He was already in love, but tonight he absolutely fell in love.

Tonight I really wanted to be with Jordan as well. Not just at the party, but I wanted to be wrapped up in his arms for the after party. He had to pick up his daughter from her Grandmother's house on his way in. So it wasn't happening tonight. He was disappointed as well that we couldn't cap the night off.

Furthermore, tonight I realized that I was in love with two men and both were good men.

We left the party so that Jordan could pick up his daughter. I trailed him to the expressway, and got off at my exit as he kept going. We talked on the phone all the while until he was sure that I made it home safety. I thought that was gentlemanly of him.

***

Several months passed. Kyder and I were now two months away from the wedding day. We were so busy running around trying to make sure that everything would be perfect. It was really coming fast and I had so many mixed emotions about the wedding, but there was no way I could back out now. The show had to go on. I was so busy that I didn't have time for Jordan during these two months. I missed him but, I had a lot to do. I just hoped he would understand and wait for me.

It was getting closer and closer to the wedding day. Jordan had begun to act funny. Even though it was killing him he stepped back to let me get through the wedding.

Jordan was hurting something awful, but there was nothing he could do about it. He only prayed that I would come back to him after the wedding. The last two weeks before the wedding we didn't see each other. We had brief conversations daily up until the Thursday before the wedding. Then after that all calls, visits and conversation ceased. The day of the wedding Jordan told me he got drunk. He drank six shots of tequila. All he wanted to do was pass out and go to sleep hoping the day would be over.

He said he had hoped for one phone call during the week after the wedding even if it was for one brief minute, but it didn't happen. He felt that one phone call would have told him that I truly loved him and was thinking about him as well. I know he felt I could have found some time somewhere because he had always told me you find time for things you want to do.

I wanted to call him so badly, but I couldn't because Kyder was all over me. His response was that he finds or make a way to call me no matter what he is doing or where he is.

CHAPTER 31

Tayla

I called Jordan Monday morning after returning from the honeymoon. I was glad to be married, but I missed Jordan so much. I knew I shouldn't be calling him, and so soon. But I needed to talk to him, to see him, to touch him.

Jordan had become a big part of my life that I couldn't let go of. If it was legal in American to be married to two men, Jordan would definitely be my second husband. For some strange reason I felt a connection with him. You know the connection as though you have children together, but we have none. Love is such a funny thing.

He sounded surprised that I called. Jordan didn't expect me back for a few more days. He was acting nonchalant on the phone. I thought he would be excited to hear from me. I'm sure he just probably didn't know what to expect from me now that I'm married. I believe Jordan didn't think I was coming back to him. I believe he had prepared himself to believe that what we had was over. Jordan told me since our last contact on that

Wednesday before I got married and the week after he went through pure hell. He said it finally got better for him by the end of the week. He convinced himself that we were over. The thought of us ending hurt him, but he was now able to deal with it.

Ending our love was the furthest thing from my mind. I needed Jordan in my life. I wasn't sure why Jordan was brought into my life, but I do know that everything in life happens for a reason.

When I called Jordan after I returned, I needed to see him and I couldn't wait another day or minute. I knew he needed to see me even though he was acting like he didn't.

"Hey I said," when Jordan answered the phone.

"You're back?" asked Jordan.

"Yes, we got back Saturday night."

"I see."

I knew there was no way he was going to ask anything about the wedding or the honeymoon. This was something Jordan wished never happened and he wanted to bury and forget about it forever.

There was a pause while Jordan was trying to think of something to say besides how everything went. He could care less if things went perfect. I sensed that he wished that it didn't, but he knew in his heart it was the most perfect wedding.

I broke the silence in the air. I wanted him to feel comfortable with me again. I wanted Jordan to know that I still loved him and he would forever be in my life as long as he would have me.

"Can I see you today?" I asked.

It was Monday and it wasn't one of the days that we normally saw each other unless it was for a quick hug or kiss if one of us needed it.

"Today? How much time do you have?" asked Jordan.

"I have an hour or so."

Jordan knew that meant I only had one hour. I know he wanted to see me, but I also knew he wanted more time to be with me then an hour. He always expressed there were too many quickies with us lately. He also felt he was getting the short end of the stick and where would all this lead us once his marriage was over. He knew he could never ask me for anything more and he knew that it would never be more then what he is getting right now. "Today." Jordan sounded like he wanted to say "No," but he couldn't. He wanted to see me even if it meant for a short period of time.

"Okay Tayla. Where do you want to meet?"

"At your spot."

When we only had an hour or two Jordan liked going to this hotel that was twenty-minutes out of our area.

"Okay, I will meet you there," Jordan finally said.

***

Later that day, I arrived at the spot first. I checked into the hotel and got our room number. I called Jordan on his cell to inform him of the number of the room. I undressed as I waited on his arrival. Shortly after turning the bed back while standing in my birthday suit, Jordan knocked on the door. I let him in and locked the door behind him.

Jordan quickly undressed.

"Damn, I don't get a kiss or a hug?" he said.

"I was giving you time to get yourself together," I responded as I got up off the bed and walked over to Jordan.

He grabbed me up in his arms as I reached up to his muscular fine body to kiss his lips.

Jordan picked me up in his arms and carried me over to the bed, as I was wondering what he had in mind for us today.

Jordan was always very creative with our love making experiences, and each one was always a challenge and experience. It was the element of surprise with him that made you want to come back for more and wished that it never end as we lived for the moment in our secret world.

Jordan's phone would always ring bringing us back to reality. Someone was always calling for his help for one thing or another. Jordan was a very skillful man. He had skills in many areas from counseling, remodeling houses, cars, working with children and of course women.

Wow! What a man.

But, there were times when I felt like I was not the only woman in Jordan's life besides his wife. I felt there were other woman that he was involved with even though I don't have any evidence to support my thinking. It was just a feeling. You know how emotions can run wild sometimes.

As I suspected. Jordan was creative as hell today. He was flipping, bending, rocking and doing all range of motions you could think of or shall I say that I never thought about.

Sometimes he made me forget about my age. I knew my body shouldn't be doing all of this kinky shit, but it was all worth it. My body told me to get a grip on myself as this man was rocking my world.

The reality of it all is that this man would never be mine and I will never be his completely. I would never have the time that he needs or wants even if he divorces his wife. That's only because I'm married now myself. I know eventually Jordan will get tired of not having me when he wants or needs me. It will only be a matter of time when he would want someone else to fill the empty void in his life. The love making that we encounter will only take us so far. There could never be more than making love with us. We could never have the dinners, the movies, and the walks in the park, or sitting by the beach and the special trips or family functions. There still will be many nights of him not being able to talk with me when he needs someone to talk to, lonely nights when he needs someone to be with or hold him, and lonely occasions when he needs company at some function or another. All I can do is try to make the best of our time that we have together as long as we both our able to deal with our secret romance.

I know at times it kills Jordan just listening to all the things and outings that Kyder and I attend together. He hasn't had that in a long time with his wife and once he is divorce he knows he still won't have it. He listens without saying a word, but I know in his heart he wished he didn't know about them.

I remembered Jordan telling me once that he has never been jealous of another man, because he can get anything that another man has if he wanted it. He stated that he is jealous of Kyder because of what we have together. He is jealous of the love we have together because he wished it was him in his shoes and he knows that we can never have the quality times that Kyder and I have.

Jordan is hanging in there for now. I wish that it would never end. In fact, he told me we will be together forever, but I know that once his divorce is final he will not be content with how things are now. He won't feel that he has to settle for what I have to offer and if I can't satisfied his whole being, not just sexually, I know that will be the end of our love.

CHAPTER 32

Tayla

I had stopped dancing at Red's once I got married. I knew there would be no way I could continue while living in the same house with Kyder. Although, I wished I could find a way to continue for a little while to begin a nice savings for myself. You never know what can happen in life. I've learned from dealing with Roscoe that a woman always needs a savings just in case she needs to leave.

Carlito told me that I could come back anytime, and if I wanted to work one or two days a week he would work something out for me. I think I might just take him up on that offer. I think I can swing one or two days a week here and there. I will never totally depend on a man's money for as long as I live. Due to Kyder's work hours I know I can manage the time I need to make the cash. The money is good and I know within two to three months I can have enough money for a nice little savings. Then maybe I will take a break and start again later. I don't think I will ever give it up completely. I have to hold on to it just in case I need it down the line.

I could also make some cash by just going to the club to talk with Mr. Zindale. I know he is still looking for someone to talk with so that he could dish out his money. Now, that was easy money. I would start that way then work my way back up to dancing. As a matter of fact, I plan on going to Red's this week to sit with Mr. Man to make some fast cash.

***

Later in the week I did just that. I dressed myself up really nice and went up to Red's on the day I knew Mr. Zindale would be there. I spotted him as soon as I walked in the door. He spotted me as well and waved for me to come over. He fell right into my plans. "Great," I said to myself as I made my way over to him.

"Hey Tayla, you're looking even good in regular clothes. Let me buy you a drink."

"Thanks."

"So I hear that you won't be dancing for a while."

"Yeah, I decided to take some time off. I need to spend some time with my daughter."

"Oh, you have a daughter?"

"Yes, she was with her father, but now she is staying back with me." I decided to be half-way honest. "I wasn't in a position to take care of her that's why I started dancing to save money to be able to take care of my daughter."

"And now, you feel you're in a better position?"

"I'm getting there, but she comes first. That's why I needed to take the time off. I do have plans on dancing a couple of times during the week. I will need the money to help support myself and my daughter."

"Well, let me help you until you feel you are ready to dance again."

"What did you have in mind?"

"Nothing more than the usual. Why don't you keep me company the days you can come out? I'm willing to pay you well for your company."

"How much are we talking about?"

"Tayla I like you. I'm willing to give you more than the usual. Let's say two thousand a night."

I almost choked. Damn, this man is willing to pay me more than I was making dancing. How could anyone pass up a deal like this?

"That sounds good. When do we start?"

"Right now."

"Boy, you mean business."

"What do we need to wait for? I enjoy your company and you are here and so am I."

I shook my head to agree with Mr. Zindale. We talked for four hours straight then he was ready to leave. He passed me the money under the table as I quickly placed the money in my purse. I was excited from the quick money I had just earned. Money for just sitting and talking.

Carlito saw me and came over to the table. He said that he wanted to talk to me before I leave. I told him I would stop by his office. I talked with Mr. Zindale for a while then I went to Carlito's office.

Carlito informed me that he had two girls that were out ill. He asked if I would fill in at the club. There was no way I could say no. If it wasn't for him and Zena I don't know how I would ever have been able to survive. It was against my better judgment, but I agreed to help Carlito out one last time this Friday night.

Kyder was working a double as usual. So, I wouldn't have to make up a lie about where I was going. My new policy is if they don't ask don't tell.

Kyder has been working many long hours at the hospital. At times it appears as though we are growing apart. It's almost as if we are losing the connection we once had. I seem to be lonely many nights even when he is home. I know he is usually tired from working the long hours at work and I'm trying to not be selfish. I have needs that need to be fulfilled in order for me to be happy. At this point in my life my needs have been placed on the back burner with Kyder. I don't think I ask for a lot, but I need someone who I can talk with. I love a good conversation. I need someone who makes me laugh, someone who I can do new or exciting things with. I want to feel like I'm that special person in their life when I'm with them. I guess I'm still looking for that dream love where you look into their eyes and you can feel that connection.

I think I like Jordan because he makes me feel all of that and he has good conversations. Jordan always holds my attention and I could talk to him for hours and not be bored. He's spontaneous, not to mention excellent in bed. I guess he has to be spontaneous because it's hard for us to plan things.

As I sit here and think about them two I know I would rather be with Jordan. He seems to have stolen my heart, but there are many things that will only allow us to remain lovers. One major reason is that we both are married now, but who knows what the future holds.

Friday came too fast. It was just a week ago when Carlito asked me for the favor. For some reason I was a little nervous about dancing today. I couldn't understand why. Because dancing had become so natural to me. I tried to get myself in the mood by turning on the music. I felt maybe if I practiced my routine I would feel a little better.

I turned on the music and danced for several hours straight. I knew I still had it in me to perform, but there still was this unsettled vibe that I was feeling. It wasn't about dancing it was something else that I couldn't figure out. I wanted to call Carlito to back out of performing, but I knew I couldn't let him down.

I decided to take a nap to relax my body and mind before it was time for me to get myself together. I turned off the music and went to my bedroom to lay down.

As I crawled up into my bed my mind began to wander. Suddenly Jordan came to mind, and my body instantly began to relax. Soft glows of light shadowed me as my body began to get warm. My heart rate instantly sped up from the joy of seeing my love, and nothing else mattered at this point. In my mind he was slowly moving closer and closer to me like the quietness of a black leopard getting ready to attack his prey. He was coming like he was hungry for my love. I could sense his presence as the aroma of his body scent lingered in my mind.

He delicately pounced onto me and the heat from his body became so intense. I sensed that he wanted to play with his prey before he went in for the kill. I closed my eyes preparing myself for what he was going to do to me.

He slowly glided on top of me and ooh! He was so strong as he excited me with so much intensity that I wanted to scream. He taunted me over and over again before my body became limp and unable to move any further. The release was so wonderful that it brought tears to my eyes.

He finally released his hold on me and disappeared as quickly as he came.

I woke up several hours later sweating, and wet from head to toe. I had just experienced the dream of a lifetime.

The thought of Jordan was always enough to place me in a relaxing mood.

I woke up from the most exciting dream I ever experienced and decided to take my shower, get dressed then head out to Red's.

***

A couple of hours later I was walking into Red's. When I walked in I noticed the place was packed. I scanned the pictures on the wall of all the ladies that were performing tonight. Then I stopped and admired the last picture on the wall. It was a picture of me. I was sure to be taking that picture with me due to this being my last night of performing forever.

Carlito spotted me and came over to speak and to give me a hug. He thanked me again for agreeing to come out. Carlito was having some heavy hitters out tonight and he didn't want to disappoint them by being short on his girls.

After my conversation with Carlito I quickly headed to the dressing room. As I entered the room Zena was getting dressed.

"Hey girl," I said closing the door behind me.

"What's up Tayla? Do you see that crowd out there tonight?"

"Girl yes. The club has really been packing them in."

"Yeah, but they are here to see you."

"See me?"

"Yes you. The word got out that you would be performing again tonight."

"Zena, I have this strange feeling."

"You'll be ok girl. Remember when you get out there it's just you and your man."

"I know Zena, but it's not a scared type of feeling about dancing."

"Stop worrying Tayla. You'll be just fine."

"I couldn't explain or describe what I was feeling so I decided to drop the conversation and get dressed. By the time I got dressed Zena was already on stage doing her performance.

Carlito had already given me the lineup. So, I knew there were two more girls before me before it was my turn to stroll out on stage.

As I was waiting my cell phone rang. I made a mental note to turn it off before I went on stage. I looked at the phone and saw that it was Jordan. I remembered he was going out with his boys tonight and he probably wanted me to meet him somewhere. I was not available tonight. So I decided not to answer the phone, but I wanted to talk to him to just hear his voice. I knew I wouldn't be able to explain or would have to lie about where I was at tonight. So I decided against answering his calls.

Jordan texted me and I still didn't respond. I decided I would talk with him tomorrow.

My turn was up now when my song came on by *Color me Bad, I want to sex you up.* I went out to do my thang as quickly as possible. I was getting down when I looked into the right corner of Red's and thought I spotted Roscoe.

I wanted to run off stage but I knew that I had to complete my routine. I searched the room again as I continued my dance.

There he was. He was sitting there smiling this sneaky grin. That made my body quiver all over. I kept trying to stay focus on my routine, but the thought of Roscoe hurting me took presence in my mind. I prayed that my song would quickly end and fifteen minutes later it was over.

I picked up the money that was lying on stage and hurriedly ran off to my dressing room hoping Zena was in there. As I entered the room it was empty and I paced the floor wishing I had somewhere to hide.

I saw the knob on the door turn and I ran to the door hoping that Zena had returned.

To my surprise Roscoe walked in and closed the door behind him. I tried to get passed him to get out of the room. He grabbed my right arm with a hold that almost broke my wrist. Then I tried to scream and he placed his hand tightly over my mouth.

"I see you have acquired some skills. I always thought you where a whore and you thought you could get away from me,"

Roscoe said through crunch teeth.

I feared for my life so I quickly searched the room for anything that could be a weapon. I spotted an old crow bar that wasn't that far from me. I knew that the only way Roscoe was going to release his hold was for me to place some kind of pain on him.

So, I bit into Roscoe hand as hard as I could. He released his grip and immediately I ran over to the crow bar. He was still standing by the door so there was no way for me to get out. I had the crow bar in hand as Roscoe was coming for me. He had the look of a raging bull on his face and fire in his eyes. I just knew I was dead. I began swinging and swinging the crow bar to keep Roscoe from me. I hit him over his head and saw blood squirt out. This really fired him up. Roscoe came at me full force and knocked me off my feet. I continued to hit him with the crow bar as he was choking me. He wouldn't release his grasp and my eyes began to roll to the back of my head as I was passing out.

I woke up to blood splattered all over me, the room, and Roscoe lying in a pool of blood.

"Oh my God! What have I done?"

I began to scream from shock and the site of seeing Roscoe dead and all busted up. It took a while for anyone to notice my screams before they came into the room.

Finally Carlito flung the door open and rushed inside. He looked at the site of the room and hurried over to calm me down. Carlito held me in his arms as I frantically cried while trying to explain what had just occurred.

Zena and several other people came into the room and instantly screamed after seeing the gruesome site before their eyes of blood and Roscoe lying on the floor. "Oh my God Rocky!"

I looked up at Zena not sure that I heard her right. She called Roscoe Rocky. Did she know him?

Zena immediately came over to me while looking over the scene. I could tell from the look on her face that she thought she understood what had actually happened.

Zena came over to me and placed her arms around my uncontrollable shaking body as Carlito stood up and walked away.

I continued to look at her trying to figure it out.

"It's over now Tayla. You don't have to worry anymore."

Someone must have called the police because we heard sirens coming.

I was shocked beyond belief that I had just killed a man. Not just any man but my ex-husband. I didn't think I hit Roscoe that hard or that many times to cause that much gushing blood that came from his body.

"Zena did you call Roscoe Rocky? Tell me how do you know him?"

The police and a camera crew rushed in. It didn't hit me until I saw the cameras.

"Oh my God! How am I going to explain dancing to Kyder and Jordan? It's going to be all over the news. I have to call them and tell them first before the news exposes me."

I was looking for my purse around the room, but the police wouldn't let me touch anything. The dressing room had become a crime scene. I was being escorted to another room to be questioned about what happened. The only thing I could remember was up to the point where Roscoe was choking me and I hit him with the crow bar. Then he came after me and began choking me. The rest went blank from there. The next thing I remembered was waking up in Carlito's arms and seeing Roscoe lying in a pool of blood.

My thoughts were what have I done? The police took my statement and informed me that they would call me if they had any more questions.

I tried to go into the room to get my purse again and was told that I could not enter the room. I mentioned to the officer that I needed my purse which was in a drawer. The officer went over to the drawer and took out my purse; he then informed me that my purse had to be searched for evidence.

I waited while I allowed the officer to search my purse.

It seemed about fifteen minutes later when I finally got my purse back.

I immediately looked into my purse for my phone. I noticed I had four missed calls. Two calls were from Kyder, and two were from Jordan.

"Damn! How am I going to explain all of this?"

Thirty minutes after checking my phone I spotted Kyder running towards me. I immediately got nervous. I was afraid that Kyder was going to leave me. In actuality I was living a double life and look where it got me.

Kyder walked over to me. He grabbed me up in his arms.

"Babe, are you okay?"

"Yes Kyder, I'm fine."

I was lost for words, not knowing how I was going to get out of this web I created.

"What happened? And what are those lies they are saying on the news about you being a stripper here?"

My stomach hit rock bottom and I thought I was going to throw up. I couldn't say a word. My mind went blank as no words would come out.

"Tayla, did you hear me?" Kyder asked as he shook me.

I stood there looking into his face as the events of tonight ran through my mind. I must have fainted because when I awoke, I looked into Kyder and the ambulance woman's face. They were picking me up to place me on a stretcher. I was being taken to the hospital.

Twenty minutes later I was being rolled into the emergency room.

CHAPTER 33

Tayla

They were keeping me in the hospital overnight for observations. I was glad because that would at least buy me some time to think about how I was going to explain this mess I got myself in. I knew Kyder and Jordan both were going to want answers. I also knew that I would have a little more time before I would have to explain things to Jordan. He wouldn't come to the hospital. Jordan would never jeopardize my relationship with Kyder no matter what. So, right now I'm going to play this role out that I can't talk about it right now as long as I can.

My mind is really muddled about what happened. It all went down so fast. The only thing I could remember was being at the club doing my routine, and then I spotted Roscoe. I got nervous and unsure about what to do. I wasn't sure if I should run off the stage or continue it out. I remembered praying that the song would end so that his big harsh eyes and that crazy look on his face would stop looking at me. I was so scared and my whole body broke out in sweat and goose bumps.

As soon as my song ended I swooped my money up and

hurried off the stage. I dashed to my dressing room and after a tap on my door Roscoe walked in. That was the last thing I remembered.

The trauma of seeing Roscoe clogged my memory to the events that happened after seeing him.

The next thing I knew was that I was waking up to Carlito bending over me. By the time I came to my senses I spotted Roscoe laying in a pool of blood with his brains splattered on the floor.

There is no way I could have overpowered Roscoe to kill him, but who else was there to blame. My mind kept taking me over and over the events trying to remember something or anything that would ajar my mind to the killing of Roscoe.

Nothing! Absolute nothing was there that could help me remember.

I noticed Kyder standing in the hallway on his phone as I looked toward the door of my hospital room. I took a few breaths to collect myself. I was tired from trying to understand it all and worried about telling the truth of what I had been doing at the club. I knew eventually the lie would come out which is why I stopped in the first place. I wanted to avoid telling them the truth about me dancing at the club. I hoped that it would never come out. Now that it did I have to deal with it. That is the disturbing thing about it all.

Kyder walked back into the room and I pretended to be asleep. He walked over to the side of my bed, grabbed my hand and kissed me on the forehead.

I slowly opened my eyes and stared up at him.

"Hey you," said Kyder.

I smiled up at him before saying, "Hi."

"I see you are still tired. I'm going to let you get some rest then I'll be back to check on you. I'm going to look in on some of my patients while I'm here at the hospital.

"Okay Kyder."

I was glad. I still had some time before I had to tell him the truth. I know there is not going to be any way of getting around it. I also know that Kyder was just giving me time before he wanted answers.

Kyder began walking out of my room as my phone ranged. It was Zena on the phone.

"Hey girl. How are you feeling?"

"I'm good Zena. I was just trying to figure out how to explain to Kyder about me being at the club, and we need to talk."

"What are you going to do?" Zena was ignoring what I just said.

"I have to tell the truth. It's time to stop lying. I have to let the chips fall where they may."

"Good Luck girl. I can't tell you what to do. You have to do what is best for you."

"Well, Zena. I think it's time for me to be honest. I don't see any other way of getting around it." I thought I would throw this in. "Honesty is the best answer don't you think?"

"Tayla you are a grown ass woman. Handle your business as you see fit. Let me know if you need me. I'm here for you as always. So when are they letting you out of that place?"

"I don't know girl. I haven't been in a hurry to go home, but now I think it's time for me to go."

"Well, give me a call when you get out of there. I'll stop by and see you."

"Okay girl. I'll call you when I get home."

"Okay later."

After I got off the phone with Zena I closed my eyes to think for a moment. I knew all hell was going to break loose when I tell Kyder that I have been dancing. I wanted to get my words together before dropping the bomb on him.

I finally drifted off to sleep after about twenty minutes. I was awaken when the doctor walked into my room.

He informed me that they were releasing me today. They couldn't find anything wrong. I was told just stress. It was the shock from the drama of dealing with Roscoe and seeing him dead. I was told to go home and get some rest.

Kyder walked in just at the moment when the doctor said get some rest.

"Don't worry about that Dr. Robinson. I will make sure that she does just that," said Kyder.

Kyder looked over at me as he made his statement.

"In that case I'm sure you're be in good hands. The nurse will be in a moment to give you your release papers."

"Okay doc. Thanks for everything."

"Not a problem. I know that Kyder is going to make sure that you follow the doctor's orders."

"You're right about that," I said. Kyder winked at me.

"Take care you guys," said the doctor as he started walking toward the door.

I quickly got up and went to the closet to get my clothes on.

"Slow down. You haven't even gotten your release papers."

"Well once they come I'll be ready to walk out the door."

"Let me help you get dressed."

"That's okay Kyder. I can get dress on my own."

"If you say so."

"I do."

"Then in that case I'm going to run and check my schedule for the surgeries I have scheduled. I will be back shortly then we can go home."

"Okay Kyder. I should be ready when you return."

I got my clothes on and waited for the nurse to return with my discharge papers. Fifteen minutes later the nurse walked into my room with the papers in hand. I signed the needed sections and the nurse gave me a copy.

Kyder returned five minutes later with a wheelchair.

"Who is that for," I asked.

"The patient at hand."

"Kyder I can walk. I don't need to be wheeled out."

"Today you're going to ride out. Now let's not argue about this. Are you ready to go?"

"Yes Kyder."

"Good then let's ride."

Kyder took me home. I was so glad to be in my own house and own bed. It's nothing like your own.

Kyder went and ran me some bath water.

I was thinking a nice hot bath and some warm pajamas would sure do a woman good.

I took my bath once Kyder informed me that he had finished preparing the water.

I soaked and relaxed in the water until the water began to turn cold. I prayed asking for strength, and got my mind right to be able to tell Kyder about why I was at the club.

Twenty minutes later I got dressed in my warm pajamas. I was prepared to do what I had to do. I wanted to get it over. I called for Kyder to come into the bedroom so we could talk. He was in his office looking over some papers.

Kyder came into the room and softly sat down on the bed.

I looked up into his handsome face and knew I was about to break his heart. The truth was going to eventually come out. I felt it would be better if Kyder heard it from me.

"Yes Tayla, what is it?"

"I have something I need to tell you."

"Okay, go ahead."

I turned my head away from him as I tried to spit out what I needed to say. I stuttered on my words as Kyder looked me in my eyes.

"Kyder, I was dancing at this club when I finally got myself together after losing my child."

"What do you mean?"

I paused for a minute afraid to continue.

"Go ahead. What are you trying to say?"

"I'm trying to tell you the reason why I was at Red's."

"Yes, I am curious about that. Why don't you tell me?"

I had to release the words that I know would destroy Kyder, but it had to be done.

"I....... was dancing that night at Red's when I spotted Roscoe in the audience."

Kyder stood up. "Again I'm asking you. What do you mean dancing?"

"I was dancing on stage Kyder."

I finally said it.

"Do you mean stripping?" shouted Kyder.

"Well not exactly stripping."

"What do you mean not exactly? Either you were or you wasn't? Did you have your clothes on Tayla?"

"We have costumes that we wear."

"Lingerie?"

"Yes Kyder." I said with my head down.

"Oh my God Tayla! But why? Why do you have a need for stripping? It can't be for the money. You have everything you want and need."

"At first it was for money. I needed the money to get a safety net for when I got Kayla back."

I began to cry, as I tried to explain my side to Kyder.

"I never wanted to be in the position I was in when I left Roscoe. I had nothing and nowhere to go. I didn't have a job or anywhere to live. I couldn't afford even a loaf of bread. So, I did what I did to survive and to get on my feet. So that I would not have to depend on anyone."

"Wait a minute Tayla, because I'm just not getting it. I can understand it in the beginning. What I'm having a problem with is now."

"Kyder I did quit. In fact I haven't danced in over a year until that night."

Kyder was angry. I could see it all in his face. The hard look he had was like he hated me right now. He swirled his arms in the air. "Then why on earth did you start back?"

"I only did it for that one night as a favor to Carlito."

"Who the hell is Carlito?"

"The owner of the club. He had been so nice to me when I was down. So I wanted to help him out. I told him that this was the absolutely last time."

"I don't buy that shit Tayla. How do I know that you quit?"

"I give you my word Kyder."

"Your word! Your word doesn't mean a damn thing to me right now. You have been sneaking behind my back stripping and allowing other men to touch and grope all over you and your body."

Kyder looked at me like he was disgusted and he could throw up.

"It wasn't like that Kyder."

He began to shout. "Don't tell me it wasn't like that! I know about those kinds of places and the things that happen there."

"Wait Kyder. Please let me."

"Let you continue to stand there and lie to me. Enough Tayla. I'm going to the hospital. I hope you made a lot of money because when I return I don't want you to be here."

"Kyder please!"

"I can't stand to be made a fool of. You have disappointed me, and you are not the woman I thought you to be. I'm going to the hospital. This conversation is done!"

CHAPTER 34

Tayla

Kyder left the house and did not return for three days. I refused to leave until I pleaded my side one last time. I know I hurt him which was never my intention.

I was standing in the living room when he walked into the house. The moment he saw me his eyes turned cold and stone.

"I thought I told you I didn't want you here when I return. I gave you three days to get your things and get out."

"Kyder can you find it in your heart to hear me out?"

"You didn't confide in me or ask my advice when you made your decision to strip. So you sure as hell don't need to talk to me now. Just leave Tayla. We have nothing to talk about."

"Please Kyder," I said crying.

"I will give you thirty days to find a place. I'm only doing this for Kayla because I don't want to see her on the street. If you are not gone in thirty days, then I will be forced to put your shit on the street. Do I make myself clear?"

I tried to touch Kyder to hold his hand. He backed away. Kyder would not even look at me any longer.

"I hear you Kyder."

I walked away to the bedroom. I sat on the bed for a moment to collect myself. I never wanted to go down this road again to allow another man to take me there. I refused to be weak again. It has to stop. At this moment I got up from my bed. I decided that today I was going to make a change. No longer would I give a man the option of putting me out. I will be in control of my life, my finances and my own place.

I was always told if you want things to change you have to start with yourself.

I wiped away the tears from my eyes. I don't want to be anywhere, where I'm not wanted even thou I do love Kyder. I admit I made a mistake and I was trying to correct it, by stopping and coming clean.

Kyder won't even hear me out. He just wants me out. So there's nothing else to do but leave.

I left Kyder before the thirty days and got a place just for me and Kayla. In the process of it all Kyder filed for divorce. He said he couldn't live with the fact that his wife was a stripper. In his mind I had been with many men while we were married. There was no convincing him otherwise.

I finally got a real job in a Nursing Home admitting patients. The legit money that I make, the money that I saved from dancing and the money I was given through my divorce will surely help me to become stable. I'm standing on my own now and doing a good job at it.

I have one more hurdle to cross. I have to go to court for the murder of Roscoe. His family is really pushing the case for me to go to jail for his death.

I know there is no way that I could have had enough strength to kill Roscoe in that way. I don't know if I will ever find out the real truth of what really happen. I just know that I didn't kill my baby daddy. Now I just have to prove it.

I also wanted to get with Zena. I have to find out what is her connection with Roscoe. The feeling that I have is not sitting well with me.

I dialed Zena's number to see if we could meet up.

"Hey Zena."

"Hi Tayla. How are you doing?

"I'm fine. Hey I wanted to know if you were busy. I was going to stop by in a few."

I'm sure Zena wanted to avoid having this conversation, but she knows that I'm not going to let it go.

"I'll be here Tayla if you want to stop by."

"Okay, I'm on my way."

I drove over to Zena's house. I couldn't wait to hear about her connection to Roscoe.

I'm sure Zena already knew why I was coming over. Once I got there I went straight into the living room. I sat down on the couch and waited for her to start the conversation.

"Tayla I know I should have told you this a long time ago, but I didn't find out until we drove over to your house that I knew Roscoe."

"And how do you know him?"

"Um….well,"

"Come on girl. Spit it out!"

"Tayla it's so complicated. You were going through a lot at the time when I discovered I knew Roscoe. It was shocking to me so I know how you would have taken it."

"Try me."

"I….."

"Come on Zena. Just tell me."

I wanted to tell Tayla but how do you tell your friend that you have been sleeping with her husband? It was more difficult to say then I thought. I know that I also helped Tayla to leave Roscoe and to get her daughter back. It was all done for her. I just hope she would see it my way.

"I stood up as I was getting ready to let the rat out. "Look Tayla I was sleeping with Rocky. I mean Roscoe. He was my man. I didn't know you were his wife at the time. I didn't realize it until I went to your house with you to get your things."

"I see now. It's all clear. That is the reason you froze when you saw him. It was not because of your past abuse. It was because you didn't want me to know that you were Roscoe's mistress?"

"Tayla it was just unbelievable that he was the same person. My man and your husband. I wanted to tell you, but you were already going through a lot at the time. I didn't know how to break the news to you."

"The same way you are doing it now would have been nice."

"I know Tayla and I wished I would have done that at the time. When I saw who he was my only thoughts were how I could help you get your child back. That was my only intention. So I continued to see Roscoe to bring Kayla home to you."

"I know Zena and that's the only reason why I'm not mad at you. I only wish you had told me when you found it out."

"I'm sorry for not telling you Tayla, but I think it was best that way. I didn't even know if I was going to be able to do it. I didn't know if Roscoe was going to fall for me spending some time with Kayla. I had to win him over and make him trust me. I did everything I did for you girl."

I calmed down because Zena was so right. She did play with fire in order for me to get Kayla back, and for that I am grateful.

"Okay girl. I forgive you."

"Thank you Tayla. I want you to know that I would have never messed around with Roscoe if I knew he was your husband. You are my friend and I will never jeopardize our friendship like that."

"I know Zena. I trust you. If you would have just trusted me with that information up front we could have worked this out a long time ago."

"I know Tayla, but your emotions were everywhere. I don't think you would have been able to handle it like you are now."

"I don't know, but I'm glad you finally told me the truth."

"Me to Tayla. So really, how are you?"

"I'm good Zena. I made a lot of mistakes in the past. Now I'm planning to do some things better and a lot of things differently. This is my motto for the new year."

"Have you heard from Kyder at all?"

"No and I don't plan to. He has too much pride to take me back. My face has been all over the news and it will be on the news again once the trial starts. Kyder doesn't want to have anything to do with me."

"And how do you feel about that?"

"It hurts, but what can I do. I did this to myself. I just have to make better choices from here on out. All of this has been a learning experience for me."

"Tayla I think you have become a better person dealing with all the drama you had to go through."

"I hope I'm a better person."

"What's up with Jordan?"

"Actually nothing. I haven't seen him in awhile. I have been trying to get myself together. He doesn't even know that Kyder and I are not together."

"What? I can't believe you haven't told him."

"No. I needed a little space to figure things out, but we will be hooking up in an hour. I will tell him about everything when we meet. So let me get going to meet this man."

"Okay Tayla. I will check with you later."

"Bye Zena," I said as I was walking out the door.

CHAPTER 35

Jordan

Tayla and I were hooking up today. There were a lot of things we needed to talk about. It had been a while as usual since I've seen her. We really haven't been spending any time together and barely talking on the phone. I had to ask myself what am I holding on for. I haven't been getting anything out of this relationship but disappointments time after time. Tayla always blamed me for us not hooking up, but there has only been a few times where it was my fault. Generally we haven't been able to hook up because of Tayla.

It's okay. It doesn't hurt like it use to. I have come to the realization that Tayla's heart is not in it like it used to be. The less and less contact has helped me to keep my emotions in control. I kept saying I wanted to take my heart back. Now it has happened.

I was driving to meet Tayla at the bar where we use to have shots and hot wings. I needed an open area to meet her. I knew if we were secluded I would want to make love to her. Then I would be putting my heart back on the line. I smiled to myself thinking about the memories we once shared. I know that when

I get old and placed into a nursing home I will have some good memories to think about. It was fun while it lasted. Now I must face facts with dignity and let go.

I made it to the bar and waited for Tayla. I knew I would be there early, because I don't like to be late for anything. I parked my car and decided to give Tayla a call to see how close she was.

"Hey where are you?"

"I will be pulling up in about ten minutes."

"Okay. I'll see you when you get here."

I decided to go ahead in and find us a seat. I wanted to get a good table where we could sit and talk.

I spotted one in the corner of the bar. I sat at the table and waited for Tayla's arrival.

She came walking in fifteen minutes later. Once she arrived I motioned for the waiter. I ordered two shots of 1800 Tequila and some hot wings.

"Hello you," said Tayla.

"Hey stranger," was all I could think to say. I didn't know how to start the conversation. It had been a while since we had been together. So I decided to take a moment to just look at Tayla. I always thought she was beautiful inside and out. I was looking so hard into her eyes. I wanted to see if I could still feel her heart.

Tayla asked, "Is everything okay?" You're starring at me."

"You tell me."

"Well I do have a lot to tell you."

"Go ahead."

Tayla got silent for a minute. "Wow, I don't know where to start."

Tayla wiped at the hair that was dangling in her face. She held her head up then said, "Kyder and I are no longer together. In fact I have moved out and he filed for a divorce."

I know I must have been looking crazy at Tayla about now. I was in total shock.

"You're kidding right?"

"No Jordan it's true."

"What happened?"

"Well."

Tayla began to stall.

"I'm so sorry Tayla."

"It's okay Jordan. I'm good with it all now. It's been three months."

"What? You mean you haven't been with Kyder in three months and you didn't tell me?"

"Jordan I needed some time to think things through. I didn't know what I wanted to do or was going to do."

"Damn baby. I just wished you would have let me be there for you."

"As I said before its okay."

"Tayla, but why? What made all of this occur?"

Tayla took my hand in her hand. I could tell she wanted to say more, but the words would not come out. I could see the tears forming in her eyes as she turned her head to hide them.

I knew I had to say something to make her feel better.

"Tayla, I'm here for you. Whatever it is let me help you get through it."

"Jordan you won't understand."

"Try me."

Tayla began to weep. I got up and sat on the same side of the table as Tayla. I moved my chair closer and placed my arm around her shoulder.

"It's okay Tayla. If you're not ready to tell me that's fine. I want you to know that you can count on me whenever you need me."

"Thank you Jordan. It's not that. It's something I have done."

"What could you have possibly done?"

"You mean you haven't heard?"

"Heard what?"

"About the incident down at Reds?"

"Tayla I very seldom watch TV. The news is to depressing, but what does Red's have to do with you?"

Tayla looked at me like she was stunned.

"When you didn't hear from me what did you think happened?"

"I thought you were really busy and you needed some time.

No, the truth is I thought you were through with me. I called your phone twice and texted you but you didn't respond that day or any other day until we set this meeting up."

"Jordan, Roscoe is dead."

"Dead?"

"Yes, I saw him at Red's. He attacked me and I hit him with a crow bar, but I don't think I hit him hard enough to kill him. He was choking me and I passed out. When I came to there was blood everywhere and he was dead."

"Oh my God Tayla. Are you okay?"

"I'm fine now Jordan. I was in the hospital for a couple of days. It was nothing but stress and the drama of dealing with Roscoe."

"What were you doing at Red's?"

Tayla lowered her head.

"I….. was one of the dancers there."

"What?"

"I was working at Reds."

"Yeah right."

"It's the truth Jordan. I was on stage dancing when I spotted Roscoe."

I moved my chair back in order to look Tayla in her eyes.

"You're not kidding?"

"No Jordan. I'm telling you the truth, but I had quit over a year ago. I was doing one last favor for Carlito."

"Unbelievable."

"I know."

"Jordan it wasn't easy telling you this but I had to tell you the truth."

"You could have told me the truth a little sooner, like over a year ago."

"I know Jordan. I'm not proud of what I did, but I needed the money. The only thing that I did was dance. There was no sex involved."

"Is that the truth Tayla?"

"Yes Jordan. That is the truth."

"Then it's okay. I understand. You did what you had to do at the time. Are you done with stripping?"

"Yes completely."

"Then we don't need to talk about it anymore."

"Thank you for being understanding, but it's not over yet."

"What do you mean?"

"I have to go to court for Roscoe's death."

"No way, that was self-defense."

"I was trying to defend myself until I passed out. I know I didn't kill Roscoe."

"Then don't worry. I'm sure you will be cleared."

"I hope so."

"Trust me. You'll be fine."

"You think so?"

"Yes Tayla. I do believe it will work out. Now tell me what your plans are now that you are no longer married."

"I have no plans. I'm taking it slow right now. I'm not going to rush into anything."

"Then what are your plans as far as me?"

"I don't have any plans even for us right now. Jordan I can't think about anything until after this case is over. Besides, you are still married."

"Not for long. Candice has filed for a divorce as well."

"I see. We still need to take it slow. Why don't we let time be our guide, and we will take it from there."

"Fair enough. So when do you go to court?"

"In a couple of weeks."

"I have faith that everything is going to work out. Don't worry."

"It's hard not to worry. I won't be able to relax until court is over, and I'm cleared."

"Keep the faith, Tayla."

Jordan and I decided to take it slow. We didn't want to rush into anything with all the things I have been going through. We remained friends and he was always there for me. He told me he would always be in my life one way or another. Jordan reminded me that we toasted to forever. That could mean friends or lovers, whichever way life takes us as long as we are connected. I was good with that for now. I needed time to get myself together before I could get involved in another relationship. Today and right now, I'm going to focus on me and Kayla. I am the key to our happiness.

CHAPTER 36

Kyder

Tayla allowed me in her life and her heart. I think I needed her just as much as she needed me. We had spent a great deal of time together and we did some traveling as well. My intentions were to show her all the finest things in life.

I believe I helped her to get out of that shell she was living in and to develop her self-worth. She appeared to be a stronger person now, and she had some goals of her own that she wanted to accomplish. Throughout it all she got her daughter back, and got a divorced from her savage husband. She has been going to church which I know has helped her in so many ways.

Tayla finally became my wife and we were a family. Everything was going perfectly well, but she at times were beginning to be a little distance. I took it as the long hours I was working at the hospital was beginning to get to her. I know how a woman needs attention, but with doctors hours it was hard to give Tayla the attention that she needed and wanted.

I loved Tayla and I attempted to show her how much I loved her. She had everything she could ever want in life, and the things she didn't have there was no problem getting them for her. I know the material things were not an issue to Tayla. As I mentioned before, she wanted my attention and I couldn't give her the attention she needed right now. It wasn't that I didn't want to. It was because of my work hours. I never planned on working more than usual. Several doctors retired and the hospital was short of doctors. So I had to put in more time. I had hoped that it would be temporally, but it was lasting too long.

Tayla asked me once before why do I have to work such long hours? She knew I didn't really need the money. I actually do need the money. I didn't want to depend on the money from my family. Even though they are rich. I'm a real man, and I can't be the man I need to be if I'm depending on someone else. The reason I went to school in the first place is to become a doctor so I won't have to depend on my family money.

But, getting back to Tayla. We were doing okay. That's what I thought.

Then the news came out about the death of her ex- husband. It happened at this club called Red's. Tayla was there when it happened. In fact she was the main suspect in his death. I couldn't understand her purpose for being there. Tayla finally admitted that she has been, "Dancing at Red's."

My wife had been a stripper right under my nose. How could I have been so blind and made a fool of? I almost lost it when she was forced to tell me the truth. I wondered if her face was never plastered over the TV would she had told me. I think not.

It was just the idea of my wife dancing and doing who knows what for all those men week after week.

Tayla doesn't realize how she made me look like such a fool. I can't even look at her anymore. The behavior that she was doing is unacceptable to me and my customs.

"Oh my God, what is my family going to think?" I had to leave her to get out of that marriage. I had to get away from her. I have never walked away from anything in my life, but there was no way I could stay married to Tayla. She gave herself to other men, and she continued to lie about it. It couldn't be for the money. We have all the money she would ever need.

There was no way I could stay after discovering what she had been doing. I could never trust her again. Every time I'm at work I would be wondering if she's stripping again. I can't live like that. I won't allow my mind to be a hostage to thoughts like is my wife being unfaithful. The trust we had is gone.

I know she is going through a lot right now. She is accused with killing her ex-husband. I can't help her anymore. I wish her the best of luck for Kayla's sake. I know there is no way she could even have the strength to kill that man, and if she did I'm sure it was self-defense.

Tayla will be cleared of that crime. I'm sure. I just felt sorry for Kayla. I wanted to be there for her so she could have a strong family environment. All children need a positive father in their life.

Tayla has destroyed any chance of us being a happy family.

I'm an up front and to the point guy. I don't play games with people or their emotions. I know that I would not be happy about what Tayla did. I could never deal with the fact that she was a stripper.

So, I left. I filed for a divorce. There was nothing more I could do for Tayla.

CHAPTER 37

Tayla

My court date arrived. I was sitting next to my lawyer shaking very nervously. I was scared that I was going to be charged with Roscoe's death. By the time the judge walked in, I had lowered my head to say a prayer. As I sat at the table waiting for my verdict to be read, I was nervous as hell.

"Mrs. Anderson will you please stand," announced the judge.

My feet felt like weights as I struggled slowly to stand. I was reminded of all the pain, suffering and abuse I endured over the years. I wondered what would become of my precious Kayla who was only three years old.

I turned and took one long look at my daughter as she sat at Zena's side. I was hoping this wouldn't be the last time I laid eyes on her.

I knew there would be no way the judge would free me from what happened to Roscoe. The realization of it all had just settled in. The thought of him abusing me night after night still lingered in my mind. The name calling, the hitting and the countless nights of rape stayed with me. The images were so vivid that I began to quiver.

"Are you okay?" asked the judge as he noticed my sweating and jittery movements. "I'm fine Your Honor. I managed to say."

"Then let's proceed. On the count of murder the jury ..."

"Wait!"

I heard someone scream out. One of the police officers ran to the front of the court room with a tape in hand.

"Your honor. I have some evidence here that will show that Mrs. Anderson didn't kill her husband."

Everyone in the court room began talking to each other.

"Quiet, quiet in the court room," announced the judge.

Counsels in my chambers," said the judge.

My attorney and the state's attorney got up and went into the judge's chambers. They were gone for about fifteen minutes. When they came out my attorney rushed over to me.

"Tayla you're innocent. You didn't kill your husband."

"I know I didn't do it, but what happened that made everyone else see this?"

"A tape was brought in to prove you didn't do it."

The judge came back into the court room and everyone arose.

Tayla Anderson all charges are being dropped on you because of new evidence. Your attorney will explain it all to you. You're free to go."

I was so excited that all charges were dropped. I began to question my attorney to find out what happened.

"The tape we looked at showed a man hitting Roscoe several times with the crow bar. You were already passed out on the floor. Roscoe was trying to undress you."

"Roscoe was going to rape me?"

"We believed he would have until he was stopped."

"We don't know. They want you to come down to the station tomorrow to view the tape."

"I can't believe it."

"Yes Tayla, you're free of all charges."

The next day I went down to the police station to view the tape. My attorney was late. So I had to wait for him. He came in forty-five minutes later.

"I'm sorry I'm late." He said.

He motioned for a police officer to inform the sergeant that we were ready. We went into a room and closed the door. Once everyone sat down they started the tape. I got very nervous as I tried to look over the attack that I was a victim of. I saw everything that happened and what Roscoe did to me. Even while I was passed out he had begun to undress me. It did appear that he was going to rape me until he was wacked over the head. This man came out of the closet. I didn't recognize him, but there was something about him. I looked again and they were telling me to really think. I was told to search my mind hard and try to remember anything familiar about the person.

I kept looking at the face of this person. Then it hit me. My attorney tried to catch me because I almost fell out of my chair.

"You remember something Tayla," he asked.

The only thing I could do at this point was shake my head.

"It can't be," I cried out.

"Do you know this person? Asked the sergeant.

"I'm not sure. It's a possibility. I haven't seen him in years."

"Who do you think it could be Tayla," asked my lawyer.

I didn't want to give up the information. If it was who I thought it could be there was no way I could turn him in. I just couldn't release the name. I couldn't.

"I'm not sure. He looks like someone I thought I knew from a long time ago, but…"

"Tayla if you know this person. You have to let us question him. Tell us his name and we will determine if he is the actual person," said the Sergeant.

"But…"

The Sergeant spoke up again, "Look Mrs. Anderson. You either give us a name or you may be charged with withholding information regarding a crime. Then the judge may give you some jail time."

I looked at my attorney and shouted, "Jail time."

We just need a name Mrs. Anderson.

My attorney said, "Tayla if it's someone you truly know and

you're trying to protect him. I will represent this person if he is actual the one on the tape."

I didn't know what to say. How could I just give him up? I looked at the tape again. I wanted to be sure. Even though he looked a little heavier, had a beard, wore a hat over his head and had on dark glasses. I could still see that he looked like he could be Bill, Zena's brother. He had saved me from Roscoe. How could I turn him in?

"Mrs. Anderson. We need a name," said the sergeant.

I looked at the faces of everyone. I knew they were not going to let me leave there without giving them a name.

"Mrs. Anderson, remember you have a daughter to think about. You need to do the right thing here or you and your daughter will be affected by this. I'm sure you don't want to spend time behind bars and away from your daughter," said another officer.

"Tayla you have to make a choice. You give up a name and you remain free or they are going to arrest you as accessory to murder," said my lawyer.

"You got to be kidding."

"They are serious Tayla," said my lawyer.

I lowered my head wishing that this all was just a nightmare. When I opened my eyes everyone was still here, and all eyes were on me.

"I said quietly, It looks like it could be my friend Zena's brother, but I'm not 100% sure. I don't think she has seen or heard from him in years. We didn't know he was in town or where he even lives. I don't think she heard from him in years.

"You mean to tell me your friend has a brother and they don't keep in touch?"

"Well. Bill writes her often. At least once a month but he never had a return address."

"Do you think she still has the envelopes from the letters?"

"Yes, she keeps all of Bill's letters."

"We need to look at them. We will call Zena and let her know that we will be stopping by her house to look at the letters. One of my officers will come to her home to pick the letters up. Then we will be in touched with you, said the sergeant.

My attorney and I left the police station. I headed to Zena's house to let her know what was going on and to pick up Kayla. I drove to Zena's house and hurriedly went inside. She told me that she had just received a call from the police. I explained to her what had happened.

"There is no way Bill would do something like that Tayla. He wasn't even in town. He usually let me know when he's coming."

"I don't know what to tell you Zena. I was not sure it was even him. It's a possibility, but I'm not 100%."

"Well I have the letters. I have no problem showing them to the police. I know my brother is not a killer."

"I agree Zena. They will see that the person is not Bill. I don't think you have anything to worry about."

"I hope you are right Tayla."

"Trust me."

Several days later my attorney called me and I was asked to meet him back at the police department. The police believed that the man in the picture was Bill. They tried to locate him in every state that he sent letters from, but they were unsuccessful. Apparently, Bill moves around quite often. He had sneaked into New York and the club like they say a thief in the night and out of town the same way. There were no traces of Bill as he was never found. He continues to write Zena letters that she keeps to herself.

Zena gave the police a picture of Bill along with the letters. They continue to believe the person was Bill. Zena told me that she was now having second thoughts about Bill killing Roscoe. After learning all this news about Bill, Zena mentioned to me that she thinks Bill may have had something to do with Eric coming up missing. She never thought about this before, but now it all makes sense to her. Eric still has not been found. It's like he just vanished. Zena feels that Bill may have been watching over her after Mama died without Zena knowing it. Zena also believe that he may have been there that day when Roscoe was attacking me. I will keep her secret because if it was Bill, he saved my life. He saved me and for that I will always be grateful to him.

Today I'm releasing the bondage that was placed upon me that was holding me captive. This hour this minute I refuse to allow anyone, anything, any emotions to have that much control over me. The only person that will control my life is God. I was abused and I also allowed myself to be abused by not letting go of the person, the pain, the feelings and the encounters that were causing so much misery in my life.

All abuse is not physical. I encountered physical, mental and emotional abuse. There were times when the encounters were good feelings to me, but unhealthy. These unhealthy feelings were abusive to my mind, body and soul.

The emotions controlled my life and kept me from making positive decisions. So today I'm breaking the chains that held my life of unhealthy emotions and encounters. I'm letting God be my guide.

Domestic Abuse:

Domestic abuse is a behavior that one person engages in to unfairly control another person. The abuse is devastating to the individual and it robs the person of health, dignity and sometimes life.

It has been reported that over one million individuals are abused each year.

Domestic abuse is also called domestic violence. Domestic abuse is of many types including emotional, sexual and physical abuse. Men are sometimes abused by partners, but domestic abuse often affects women. Domestic abuse can also happen in heterosexual or homosexual relationships.

It may not be easy to identify domestic abuse at first. Some relationships are clearly abusive. They may start out subtly and gets worse over time. You may be experiencing domestic abuse when someone:

- Calls you names, insults you or puts you down
- Prevents you from going to work or school
- Stops you from seeing family members or friends
- Tries to control how you spend money, where you go and what you wear
- Acts jealous or possessive or constantly accuses you of being unfaithful
- Gets angry when drinking alcohol or using drugs
- Threatens you with violence or a weapon
- Hits, kicks, shoves, slaps, chokes or otherwise hurts you, your children or your pets

- Forces you to have sex or engage in sexual acts against your will

- Blames you for his or her violent behavior or tells you that you deserve it

Examples:

- Physical- slapping, pushing, hitting, kicking, biting, etc.
- Emotional- name calling, putting down, insults, etc.
- Sexual- being forced into sexual contact
- Threats- "If you…… I'll kill you!"
- Intimidation- gestures, looks, smashing things
- Isolation- being kept from seeing or talking to others, not allowed to go out
- Economic- being given an allowance not allowed to have a job, etc.

There are some times when domestic violence begins or increase during pregnancy, and your health and the baby's health are at risk. The danger continues after the baby is born. Even if your child isn't abused, simply witnessing domestic violence can be harmful. Children who grow up in abusive homes are more likely to become abusers or think abuse is a normal part of a relationship.

If you continue to stay in an abusive relationship it could have an effect on your self-esteem. You may become depressed and anxious. You may wonder if you can truly care for yourself or even wonder if it's your fault. You may feel helpless or paralyzed.

What you can do to break the cycle:

- Start by telling someone. It can be a friend, relative, doctor or close contact.

Leaving that person can be dangerous. Consider these steps:

- Call a women's shelter or domestic violence hotline for advice. Make the call at a safe time when the abuser is not around or from a friend's house or other safe location.
- Pack an emergency bag that includes items you'll need when you leave, such as extra clothes and keys. Hide it or leave the bag with a friend or neighbor.
- Keep important papers, money and prescription medication handy so that you can take them with you on short notice.
- Know exactly where you'll go and how you'll get there, even if you have to leave in the middle of the night.
- Use your phones cautiously- your abuser may listen to your conversation. He or she may check your cell phone to see who has called or texted you. They may also check billing records for your phone.
- Use your home computer cautiously as well- Your abuser may use or install spy ware to monitor your e-mail and the websites you visited. Consider using a computer at work, the library or at a friends' house to seek help.
- Frequently change your e-mail password. Choose a password that would be impossible for your abuser to guess.
- Clear your viewing history- Follow your browser's instruction to clear any record of web sites or graphics you've viewed.

In an emergency call 911

The following resources can also help:

- National Domestic Violence Hotline -800-799-7233
  Call the hotline for crisis intervention and referrals to
  resources, such as women's shelters.

- Your doctor- Doctors and nurses will treat injuries and
  may refer you to safe housing and other local resources.
- Local women's shelter or crisis center- Shelters and crisis
  centers typically provide 24 hour emergency shelter as
  well as advice on legal matters and advocacy and
  support services.
- A counseling or mental health center- Counseling and
  support groups for women in abusive relationships are
  available in most communities. Be wary of advice to seek
  couples or marriage counseling. If violence has escalated
  to the point that you're afraid, counseling is in adequate.
- A local court- Your district court can help you obtain a
  restraining order that legally mandates the abuser to stay
  away from you or face arrest. Local advocates may be
  available to help guide you through the process.

Women's Rural Advocacy Program

Mayo Foundation for Medical Education and Research 1998-
2010.

www.ingramcontent.com/pod-product-compliance
Lightning Source LLC
Chambersburg PA
CBHW070314260626
47160CB00003B/833